Bittersweet Chocolate

MARTHA REYNOLDS

DEDICATION

For my mother

ACKNOWLEDGMENTS

Thank you to the following people, all of whom played an important role in making this story the best it could be:

Bob Ferreira, Assistant Vice President for Alumni Relations at Providence College, and Dr. Hugh Lena, Vice President for Academic Affairs, also at PC, for their assistance in helping me understand tenure and 'financial exigency.'

Francine LaSala, author, editor, friend – your brilliant and creative mind is extraordinary.

Blanche Marriott, whose technical expertise saved me weeks of torture. Lyn Stanzione of StanzAloneDesigns, for creating the gorgeous cover to this book.

Lynne Radiches, whose feedback is always kind, constructive, and helpful. That's why you're such a good friend.

Sue Koehler-Arsenault, your intimate knowledge of Huntington's Disease helped me to understand the complexities and devastation that accompany it, and your assessment and observations of my writing about the disease were very much appreciated.

To the readers of Chocolate for Breakfast and

Chocolate Fondue: You're the reason I wrote this third and final book in the series. I can't thank you enough for the positive comments and love you've expressed to me personally and in your reviews.

And, of course, my James.
The sun in my winter sky.

Chapter One

Lausanne, Switzerland

The first time it happened was the day before Karl Berset's sixtieth birthday. He had a ten-minute walk from his office at the bank to his house on the Rue du Midi. The air was bracingly cold for late November. Maybe the sight of the Evian Mountains gleaming shiny white across the lake had distracted him. Karl caught the scent of roasting chestnuts as he passed the train station, where men with open-fire braziers still used newspaper to make cone-shaped holders for the hot chestnuts. As he made his way home in the fading light, he stopped, looked around, and couldn't remember the way. He paused, confused and unsure, and tried to remember the name of his street. Pressing gloved fingertips to his forehead, he concentrated. *This is ridiculous. I've lived on the same street for years.*

"Karl, *salut!*" He spun around to see the familiar face of Oskar Rossy, his neighbor.

"Oskar!" Karl gripped his arm, as if they were friends meeting again after many years. "So good to see you!"

"Heading home?"

"Yes, yes, I'm heading home. Let's walk together," Karl said.

"Are you all right, Karl? You seem to be out of breath."

"No, no, I'm absolutely fine. Come, let's go," Karl said, eager to be home, in his house. He was probably just tired, he thought. No need to mention it to Ella. Things between them were good these days, and he didn't want to upset her.

He waved goodbye to Oskar and opened the front door to his house. *This is my house. At least I know my own house.* A tantalizing aroma of thyme and garlic greeted him and he inhaled deeply. Ella approached from the kitchen.

"Hello, my love," she said, wiping her hands on a towel and offering her cheek for a kiss.

He kissed her mouth instead. "It smells good in here. Are you roasting a chicken for me?"

"I am. Tomorrow we go out for your birthday, so tonight I make your favorite meal." She stroked his cheek with warm, soft fingertips. "You are as handsome as you were on the day we met, Karl. Turning sixty should not concern you at all."

Sixty years old. Karl wrapped his arms around his wife's still slim waist and pulled her close. His heart was full of gratitude and affection for this woman. Ella, who had forgiven him and taken him back into their home. The mother of his children - Paul, married now and starting his own family, and Dani, his darling girl, working as a fashion model in Geneva. His life was good.

There was another child, of course, presumably living in Switzerland, the one he'd fathered with Bernadette Maguire thirty years ago. He'd given up his search after the mess with that Greek girl five years back. And he'd promised Ella that all of it was in the past. The child had not sought him out, and Karl was satisfied to leave the entire matter behind him.

"We are ready to eat in five minutes," Ella said, easing out of his clutch.

"I'll wash up." Karl turned to his right, toward the small bathroom, and bumped into the wall. "*Merde!*" He let loose with a string of expletives.

"Karl!" Ella rushed back to him. He saw the shadow of fretful anxiety in her eyes. "What is it?"

"Nothing," he muttered. "I just hit my shoulder. It was stupid." He shook his head. "I don't know, Ella." Forgetting the way home earlier had shaken him, more than he wanted to admit. He couldn't explain it away.

"Is something else bothering you, *cheri*?"

"No. Let's eat this meal you prepared," Karl said with a tremor in his voice. "Tonight we have a quiet meal and then I will go to bed and rest. I'm probably just very tired."

"Of course, my love," Ella said. She turned back to the kitchen as Karl entered the bathroom to wash his hands. He glanced up at his reflection and noticed the slightest twitch under his left eye.

***

Fribourg, Switzerland

Jean-Michel Eicher arrived for work earlier than usual. His boss had requested a meeting at eight, and Michel wanted time to check messages, perhaps enjoy a cup of coffee, and ensure that there had been no incidents the previous night. For over six years now, he'd been a loyal employee at the Hotel de la Rose in Fribourg. His career was solid and his family was growing. Life was mostly good.

Michel and Lucia now had two sons - Jean-Bernard, who was almost six, and his brother Luca, three. Both boys favored Lucia in looks, Michel thought with a smile, although Luca surely had *il diavolo* in him at times. Lucia was devoted to his mother, Klara, more than she was to her own mother, who rarely visited. Michel's father Bruno had been living with Alzheimer's disease for two years now, and Lucia did as much as she could to assist Klara, providing emotional support and comfort to her as she struggled to keep Bruno from wandering off, as he had done a few times. Klara was adamant, she did not want to put Bruno in a facility, but there were concerns. Back in June, Bruno walked away from the house wearing only his pajamas, and was found three hours later hiding in a barn nearly a mile away. After that incident, Michel installed special locks on the doors. Klara, Michel, and Lucia had keys. Little Jean-Bernard was in school now, and Lucia found a day care for Luca from ten in the morning to three in the afternoon. It gave her time to help Klara with housework and shopping, or to stay with Bruno on the rare occasion when Klara left the house.

Michel sipped coffee from a cardboard cup at the front desk and waited for his employee to arrive. He thought back to the time when Nani Karas worked at the hotel. It was five years ago, he recalled, and oh, how badly everything had turned out in the end. She'd never contacted him after leaving the hotel abruptly to return home to Greece. A few months after she'd left, he'd run into Alain Bouchard outside the hotel, and the two of them had climbed the hill to the bus station. Alain filled him in on what had happened. Nani had traveled to Lausanne to find and meet Michel's birth father. He recalled Alain saying, "I suppose she thought she was helping. If you want to know him, Michel, I can provide the contact information." Michel remembered shaking his head when asked if he wanted Alain to reveal the man's identity. "No," he had said at the time, "I have a father already, Alain. If this man chooses to contact me, I can't stop him. But I have no interest in meeting him. And if you have a way to relay that message, please do so." Alain said he understood, and from time to time, he still stopped in to the hotel to say hello to Michel. Poor Alain, Michel thought, he had invested everything he had in that relationship with Nani, and here he was, still alone. Alain had said, "She broke my heart, Michel. And you can't love like that twice."

Michel's phone buzzed next to him with a new text. Just as he flipped it up to read the message, Robert sauntered through the lobby, ready to start his shift. He pulled off his knit cap, and what little hair he had left on his head stuck up straight, filled with electricity. Michel suppressed a grin.

"*Bonjour*, Michel!" Robert raised his hand in greeting as Michel read his message.

"*Salut*, Robert," Michel replied. "I have a meeting to attend. I'll just be in the conference room if you need to reach me, but don't contact me unless it's an emergency, do you understand?" Robert needed explicit instructions, but he was a good worker, and Michel had fought for him on more than one occasion when the boss questioned whether to keep him around.

"Okay, Michel," Robert said.

Michel waited at the elevator and wondered what this important meeting was about. He had no idea that the information he was about to receive would change his life in ways he could never have imagined.

***

New York, New York

Gary Baptista had a sleepless night. Again. He'd crept into bed after midnight, trying not to disturb Bernie, who snored lightly but didn't wake when he lowered himself onto their mattress. He was half-awake when she rose, early, but turned his back to the window's light and fell into a deeper sleep. When he opened his eyes again and looked at the clock next to the bed, it was almost ten.

"Hey, sleeping beauty," Bernie said to him as he walked out of the bedroom. She closed her laptop.

He rubbed his face. "Why did you let me sleep so late?"

"Because you needed it, love." She poured coffee and handed him a mug. "You were up so late last night."

"Couldn't sleep."

"Any special reason for that?" Bernie cracked two eggs into a bowl and whisked them with a fork before sliding them into a hot skillet. She pushed two slices of bread into the toaster and waited for the eggs to set before she scrambled them.

Gary buried his face in the big mug and inhaled. How he loved his morning coffee. And how he didn't want to tell her about the meeting he'd had yesterday with the Chair of the Foreign Languages Department.

"Just a lot going on this semester," he said. He didn't look up; she'd know instantly if she looked in his eyes. Gary couldn't hide anything from his Bernadette. He'd tell her the news once he had a plan in place.

"Okay, babe. If I can help, let me know." Bernie scraped the scrambled eggs onto a plate, laid the toast alongside them, and placed the plate in front of him. He reached for the butter as she kissed his head. "I have a meeting at eleven-thirty." She disappeared into their bedroom to change her clothes.

For Gary, it was the best thing in his life when Bernie Maguire decided to move in with him. That was over five years ago, and he wouldn't have changed anything in those five years. He'd proposed to her, twice. The first time, three days after she'd unpacked her belongings and nestled them among his, she had said they should talk about it, and they never really did. A month later, he asked her again, and that time they did talk. Two months after that, on a Friday afternoon in September, they were married. Bernie's family, which consisted of her aunt Joan, her sister Joanie, her brother-in-law Lou, and her nieces Mandy and Angie, drove down from Rhode Island. Gary's kids, Justin and Nicole, were there, too, and Bernie and Gary hosted a lovely dinner celebration at Valbella. Life was good, Gary reflected.

Bernie reappeared, looking like an attorney.

"Look at you, all smart and lawyerly," he said with a grin. He piled the last of the eggs on a remaining scrap of toast and popped it all in his mouth.

She ran her fingers through his thick hair. "Take a shower and get dressed, my man. I'll see you later tonight." She bent at the waist and kissed him on the mouth. He put his hand at the back of her neck and held her there for a second longer before releasing her.

"Love," she called at the door.

"Love," he replied.

Chapter Two

"Happy Birthday, darling," Ella purred into Karl's ear before the sun had found its crooked way through the window to his pillow.

Karl reached for her in the early light, her body warm and familiar. After a restless night, he wanted nothing more than to call in sick to work, perhaps sleep a little longer. His focus had been fuzzy lately, and he'd have liked a day away from the office, but the banking industry was too volatile these days. He couldn't afford to be away *or* unfocused. From the bits of office gossip that swirled by him like wisps of smoke, he'd heard that the small bank where he'd worked since 1980 was about to be swallowed by one of the bigger three.

"Would you make an omelet for me, *cherie*?" He kissed her neck. "Since I must go to work. But you know I would rather spend my birthday right here, in this warm bed with you beside me." His left foot twitched under the sheet and he kicked her in the shin.

"Are you booting me out of bed now?" She

laughed and rolled away from him. Karl clasped his hands together under his head and watched her rise. Her skin was like milk. She slipped into a red silk robe and tied it at the waist.

"Breakfast will be ready when you're showered and dressed, old man." She blew him a kiss over her shoulder.

Karl lifted the covers and looked at his foot. Nothing. He sat up and swung his legs over the edge of the bed, and stared at his feet, hovering inches above the carpeted floor, but neither foot moved. He walked to the bathroom and started his morning ritual. It's nothing, he told himself. I'm sixty today; everything slows down a little.

Ella prepared an omelet with bits of leftover ham and mushrooms, and served it on a plate with toasted bread. Karl gazed down at his breakfast and thought again what a lucky man he was.

"I will come to your office and we'll take the train to Geneva. Five o'clock, *cheri*? Dani will meet us at the station." She poured strong, hot coffee into two small cups and slid one to her husband.

"And what about Paul and Sophie? Will they join us? Or does he have an excuse not to see his father today?" Karl stirred cream into his coffee and raised his eyes to Ella.

"Tonight they have to keep the shop open late. Most of their customers come at night, you know. He was very sorry, Karl," Ella said, avoiding his gaze.

Karl knew that Paul would stop by the

house, probably during the day when he knew his father wouldn't be home. He'd leave a calendar or a tie, something purchased and wrapped by Sophie. Karl had tried, he really had. He'd offered to help Paul find a job in the bank, but Paul wanted nothing to do with it, or with anything Karl might suggest. Paul and Sophie ran a tattoo and piercing shop in Lausanne. They lived above the shop, in a run-down apartment barely large enough for the two of them, let alone any children. Karl suspected Ella slipped him money every week.

But Dani, his Dani. His beautiful girl. She worked as a model in Geneva for a high-fashion organization. He kept asking her when she'd be in a magazine, and she would toss her pretty head and laugh. I'll let you know, Papa, she'd told him. Karl wanted to bring the magazines into work, show her off to his colleagues. Dani wore clothes from some of Italy's most exclusive designers. He was so happy she had time this evening to meet them for dinner.

"You feel better today, *cheri*? After a night's rest?"

Karl looked up at his wife. "I will call the doctor, love. Make an appointment. It's time for a physical, anyway. No reason to concern yourself. Everything is perfect."

***

When Jean-Michel stepped into the conference room on the second floor, Monsieur

Rosolen was already seated, with a pale green spreadsheet laid out on the table in front of him. Two men, unfamiliar to Michel, sat at the far end of the table, their heads close in conversation. Michel felt a wave of nausea bubble up from his stomach. Was he about to be fired? Please, no, he implored silently. Lucia was pregnant again; she'd just told him last week, but they hadn't said a word to anyone yet, not even his mother. It was early, and Klara's thoughts were consumed with Bruno, anyway.

"*Bonjour*," Michel said, nodding to the two men at the other end, who stopped whispering and looked up. "I'm sorry, am I late?"

"Not at all, Michel," Monsieur Rosolen replied. He put down his pencil and turned to the other men. "Please, why don't we all sit together?"

The men pushed their chairs back at the same time. They rose and approached Michel and his boss. Michel offered his hand. "Jean-Michel Eicher, pleased to meet you both." He looked each of the men directly in the eye. He wouldn't let them see his apprehension.

"Gamil Almazi," said the taller of the two. He had a nearly indiscernible accent, thick black hair and a goatee, and eyes black like onyx beads.

"Burt McDonald," said the other. A round, pink face, and a sweaty hand. American, Michel guessed. He actually smiled.

American and Arab, thought Michel. What's going on here? They all took seats, Almazi directly across from Michel, the American

McDonald opposite Monsieur Rosolen, who cleared his throat before speaking.

"Michel, these gentlemen are with Almazi Holdings. They arrived in Zurich the day before yesterday and stayed in our hotel last night. The company owns a number of upscale hotels."

"We are a publicly-listed holding company based in Saudi Arabia," said Almazi. "We invest in many international companies, but have recently expanded to purchase hotels."

"Most of the hotels we own are in the Middle East," added McDonald. Michel nodded, still unsure of the purpose of this meeting. He looked to Monsieur Rosolen.

"Michel, Almazi Holdings has purchased this hotel. The agreement was signed earlier this morning."

Michel stared at his boss as he felt his cheeks burn hot. He knew he was about to lose his job. Remain calm, he instructed himself silently. He swallowed hard and cleared his own throat before speaking.

"Am I out of a job?"

All three men laughed. Michel stared at them in turn. When they saw his face, they all stopped. McDonald shifted in his chair and pulled a white handkerchief from his breast pocket. He shook it out and mopped at his shiny forehead.

"No, Jean-Michel, quite the opposite," said Almazi in a neutral voice. "We know the quality of your work, and your boss here has nothing but praise for you." Michel looked to Monsieur

Rosolen with a small smile. Almazi continued.

"We'd like you to manage one of the hotels we've recently purchased in Geneva. It's one of the city's oldest hotels, and a landmark on the lake. We need a top-notch manager - you. We'll assist with moving your family, help you to find a residence, and," he slid a piece of paper across the table to Michel, "we're offering you an increase in salary."

Michel looked down at the paper. Yes, that was definitely more money than he was making now. But Geneva? What about his parents? Lucia won't want to move. He didn't know what to say.

"Of course you'll want to think about it. Talk it over with your wife and let Monsieur Rosolen know tomorrow morning. But we hope you'll join our team," McDonald said. He stood up and offered his pudgy pink hand. Michel stood and shook it, and Almazi's hand as well. He was still unable to come up with anything to say.

"We're off then." Almazi checked his watch. "Our train to Lucerne leaves at ten, and we know the train is always on time!" He laughed out loud and McDonald laughed too, following his lead. Almazi picked up his briefcase as McDonald snapped his shut.

"Thank you, gentlemen, and enjoy the rest of your time in Switzerland," Monsieur Rosolen said, escorting them out of the conference room and to the elevator.

Michel sank into his chair and pressed the heels of his hands into his forehead. Geneva! He looked at the piece of paper again. With another baby on the way, they would need the money. And he'd have to move his parents to Geneva, too. Maybe find an apartment or a small house for everyone. He squeezed his eyes shut. It can't be a small house, he thought, not if his parents come with them. Oh, this is going to be a difficult conversation tonight.

He pulled out his phone and composed a text to Lucia. *Try to get the boys to bed early tonight. I want to be alone with you.* He hit 'send.' The rest would have to wait.

Within a minute, he had a reply. Your parents are coming to dinner tonight. I just asked her. We will have to be alone later!

OK, he typed back and turned his phone off.

***

Gary walked to work whenever he could. And today was a perfect November day: clear and sharp, as if this area of Manhattan had been scrubbed clean of the grime and dust so prevalent in the city. He ambled past Jackson Square and down Greenwich Avenue, and the twenty-minute walk gave him time to think.

With declining enrollment in German studies, Gary was informed yesterday by the provost that there'd be no more German Department after the fall semester ended, meaning next month after finals. He'd been teaching German since the late eighties, for crying out loud. His pay was decent, and his benefit package was excellent. Bernie worked independently, so those benefits were necessary. What the hell was he going to do now? He'd just turned fifty; no one would be interested in hiring him. Damn it. He'd have to start looking for another job.

Justin would finish at Syracuse in the spring, and Nicole had decided that two years in the cooking school was enough. Both kids had good jobs lined up: Justin in Albany and Nicky's internship was about to turn permanent. Gary was grateful for that, and if a job meant moving, he'd be able to, but Bernie loved being in the city. If he couldn't find a position at the same salary he was making now, they'd never be able to afford their apartment.

German. He loved the language, everything about it, but lately he'd regretted not adding another language to his arsenal. Maybe Arabic or Chinese. His Spanish was passable, but he couldn't teach it, not at the college level, anyway.

He arrived at his office and unlocked the door. His one class that afternoon wasn't until two. He locked the door and fired up his computer. Screw them, he thought, I need to job hunt.

He brewed a pot of coffee and began searching for job openings. An adjunct assistant professor of German at a community college in Kansas. A part-time instructor of German in Georgia. And an assistant professor of German and French in a place called Twisted Oak Falls, Texas. Not a promising start, he thought.

"Come on!" Gary yelled at the screen. "Are

you kidding me?" There was a knock on the door. "Just a minute." He shut down the program and opened the door.

"I'm sorry, Dr. Baptista, I know it isn't your normal office hour time, but I really need to talk with you."

Sara Duffy stood in the doorway. She brushed away a long strand of dark hair and Gary noticed her hand was very small. Her fingernails were short and painted black, or very dark blue, he couldn't tell.

"Come on in, Sara. You want coffee? I just made some." Gary pulled a chair to the side of his desk.

She reached into her backpack and retrieved a slim can. "I'm fine," she said. She popped open the top and set it on his desk. Sugar-free Red Bull. Of course, he thought, remembering seeing recycle bins full of the blue-and-silver cans. All the students drank this stuff.

"What can I do for you?" He sipped his coffee.

"I need to withdraw from your class. I know I'm gonna fail it."

Gary scratched his neck. "Sara, it's too late to drop this class. Let me pull up your file." He turned to his computer and began typing. She leaned forward and laid that small hand, with the black fingernails, on his arm.

"Please," she whispered, and ran her hand up and down his bare skin.

Gary pulled his arm away and rolled down the sleeve of his cotton shirt. Buttoning the cuff, he stood, edged around her chair, and opened his office door as wide as it would go. He sat back down and gave her a pointed look. Sara lowered her eyes and Gary turned back to his computer.

"Right now, you've got a 'C,' Sara," he said, his voice a monotone. No inflection. Absolutely no emotion. "You can raise it to a 'B' if your final paper and exam are better." He removed his glasses and used his index finger to rub the spot between his eyebrows. It wasn't the first time a student had tried to flirt her way to a better grade. "I can refer you to one of our tutors if you want." He stared her down.

"I don't suppose you'd do any tutoring?" She kept her chin down and looked up at him, and he tried not to laugh. These girls, he thought. Too many movies and television shows about college professors and co-eds. She'd just picked the wrong guy.

"Afraid not. Well, I have to prepare for class, Sara, so if you'll excuse me." He pushed his chair back and stood, extending his palm to the open door. Sara frowned and stood as well.

"I should have taken Italian," she muttered and trudged out of his office.

Gary exhaled. He shut the door and locked it again. Maybe it really *was* time for a new career; he was getting too old for this.

Chapter Three

Karl Berset made it through the day at work without forgetting his name, but he did find hard to concentrate. The episode yesterday was just a fluke, he told himself, and almost believed it. He was sixty years old, had survived a heart attack, and was just six months away from retirement. By May of next year, he'd be done with the day to day annoyances of office work. He wanted to take Ella somewhere special, a way of showing her how much he appreciated her. And her forgiving, compassionate heart. Maybe a long cruise around the Mediterranean. A month in Spain, perhaps.

At three o'clock, he was summoned out of his office and greeted by his co-workers with coffee and cake. He looked at his colleagues, assembled around a table at the far end of the office. Some of the men he'd worked with over the years had retired already. Two of them, older than he, had died. The girls in the office were all young, except for Carmen at the front desk, who was ancient. She always said they'd have to carry her body out of the building. Poor thing, he thought, this place was the only family she had.

"Thank you all very much," he said. He stuck his hands in his pockets and looked at the young faces, full of promise and optimism. Some of them had been hired in the past couple of years; they wouldn't remember the way he used to be, unless others had told them. "When I was your age, I couldn't see ahead this far. Age sixty was so distant. But time passes a lot faster than you realize." He stopped, felt his throat tighten. "Don't waste a single day. Work hard, save your money, enjoy some vacation time very now and then." He stared at the table. *Don't be so dramatic*, he scolded himself silently.

"And by all means, eat cake whenever possible." The little group laughed and one of the girls stepped forward to cut slices for everyone.

A few minutes before five o'clock, Karl stood outside his office, chatting with one of his colleagues, and he saw Ella enter the building. She was just as beautiful as she was the day they'd married. She didn't see him watching her. Carmen stood to greet her and Karl leaned against the doorframe, his arms folded across his chest. Ella puts them all to shame, he thought. My wife is prettier than these twenty-year-old girls.

Carmen held out her hand to Ella, who took it in both of hers. She glanced to the back and caught Karl's eye. When she smiled, Karl raised his palm and ducked into his office. He shut down his computer and popped a mint into his mouth. Within minutes, he emerged, straightening his jacket and tie, and strode to the front area. He kissed his wife.

"You are lovely, my darling," he whispered into her ear.

He smiled as her cheeks grew pink, and he turned to wish Carmen a pleasant evening as they left the office and walked toward the Lausanne train station.

"I can't wait to see our Dani," he said, tucking his wife's arm into his own.

Karl tripped on the curb leading to the train station, but he didn't fall to the pavement, thanks to the grip Ella had on his arm, although he almost brought her down with him.

"Karl! Are you all right?"

"Yes, yes, *cherie*, I'm fine. It was nothing," he added, glancing behind him. "I simply caught my toe on the curb. It happens all the time."

"Did you make an appointment with the doctor?"

He shook his head as they resumed walking.

"I know today is your birthday. But tomorrow, no excuses. You should have your check-up."

"Dr. Piery retired. His replacement is some young kid doctor," he said, a lame attempt at lightening the mood.

She stopped walking and turned her face to his. Her look was stern and tight. "It doesn't matter. You still need an annual physical. Promise me that you will call him tomorrow."

Karl kissed his wife and touched his gloved fingertip to her nose. "I promise."

***

Michel arrived home just as the rain began. He ran the last fifty yards as water poured from the pewter sky. This morning the sun was high and pale, but clouds had moved in quickly from the mountains, as they often did in Fribourg.

He loved his parents, and enjoyed seeing them when he arrived home from work, but wished that for this one night they weren't there, in his home. He needed to talk with Lucia about the meeting, and the job offer he'd received earlier in the day. And he had no idea how she would react to the news.

"*Salut*, Michel," she said in greeting as she took his coat and hung it on a wooden peg. She turned her face up to his for a kiss. Michel leaned in to kiss her and whispered in her ear, "Let's not keep them here too long tonight."

Lucia's eyes darkened with desire. "Michel! I want to be with you, too, but we will not feed them and throw them out! Now go wash your hands and come back to see your mother." She let her fingers play on his shoulder before turning back to the kitchen. Michel craned his neck and saw his parents sitting in the living room: his father a statue, expressionless, with vacant, empty eyes that stared at nothing, and his mother, who held Luca on her lap while Jean-Bernard played with a toy truck on the floor. *How will I ever convince them all to uproot themselves from this place and move to Geneva?*

After washing up and trading his jacket and

necktie for a pullover sweater, he greeted his parents and children.

"Mama, *salut*," he said, bending to kiss her cheek. He kissed his father as well, and Bruno lifted his eyes to look at the son he didn't recognize anymore. Michel stroked his father's head, but there was no sound, no smile.

He lifted his oldest son in his arms. "Jean-Bernard, you are getting so big! Soon I won't be able to lift you anymore," he said. His son giggled in reply and threw his arms around his father's neck.

"How was your day today, my son?" Klara rocked Luca from side to side as the little boy's eyelids drooped with sleepiness.

"Fine, Mama, just fine," Michel said in a subdued voice.

"Come to table, please, everyone," Lucia called. She placed a large oblong dish on the table. Michel set his son down and followed her back to the kitchen, where he found fresh bread and salad waiting. He brought both to the table while Klara settled Bruno into a chair, then tied a clean cloth around his neck to catch the inevitable spills. Jean-Bernard climbed onto his chair, but Luca, it seemed, was more inclined to nap through the meal. Lucia laid him on the sofa where she could still see him, and covered him with a light blanket.

"Nonno has a bib just like Luca!" Jean-Bernard grinned at his grandfather, who stared back at him blankly. Klara patted the little boy's head and smiled sadly.

"Michel, will you serve? I'll do the salad," Lucia said with a pointed look at her husband.

Michel used two spoons to grasp slices of pork, chunks of potatoes, and bundles of green beans wrapped in bacon, and filled plates. He put a small amount on Jean-Bernard's plate and slid it toward Lucia, who proceeded to cut the food into tiny pieces. Klara did the same with Bruno's food.

"So, just an ordinary day, Michel?" Klara asked between mouthfuls.

"Busy," Michel replied and shoveled more food in his mouth. He hoped his mother would find something else to talk about. Michel glanced at his wife, who was focused on getting Jean-Bernard to eat. He couldn't say anything about the meeting, not at the dinner table, not without speaking with Lucia first.

Bruno grunted, and trailed his fingers through his food. Klara slid her chair closer to him and began to feed him, leaving her own dinner untouched.

"Jean-Bernard, tell your Papa what you saw today," Lucia said.

"A doggie!" the little boy exclaimed. "Her name was Hippy. Please, Papa, can we have a doggie?"

"Absolutely not!" Michel even surprised himself with the explosiveness of his reply. Upon seeing his son's crestfallen face, he softened. "Not right now," he added. "This isn't a good time."

"I thought it might be a perfect time, Michel," Lucia said softly, while giving her husband a hard look.

"No, it's really not," he said, stabbing a piece of pork.

"Boys and dogs belong together," Klara said.

Michel took a sharp intake of breath. Damn it, he thought, they're going to force this. He set down his fork. "I was offered a job in Geneva today," he blurted out. Well, there it was. He couldn't take it back now.

There was utter silence around the dinner table. Even Jean-Bernard seemed to know to be quiet. Michel closed his eyes. When he opened them, everyone, even his addled father, was staring at him. He set his jaw.

Lucia laughed. "Well, that's ridiculous! How long did you wait before turning it down?"

Michel swallowed down the bile that had risen in his throat and turned to face her. "If I don't accept it, I may lose the job I have." He heard a tiny cry escape from his mother. "The hotel was bought out." He looked at Klara. "By an investment firm, I don't know. They want me to manage a big hotel in Geneva. The implication was that I should take the job. They said they would help with moving, finding a new place to live." He lowered his eyes. "It's a lot more money."

Bruno grunted again, but stared off into space.

"I can't believe this," Lucia said, glancing at Luca, who was fast asleep in the living room. "And that you would simply announce it here during dinner, Michel." She glared at him and turned away to help Jean-Bernard finish his meal.

***

After Gary's one class ended that afternoon, he stayed around, in no hurry to walk home. He strolled to the cafeteria to pick up a sandwich and ran into Hugh Lanctot, from the French Department.

"Gary, good to see you. How's everything?"

So Hugh didn't know, or was pretending he didn't know. Gary surveyed the sandwiches wrapped in plastic and wondered how fresh they were. Hugh selected some sort of wrap. "You eat those a lot?" Gary asked him.

Hugh held up the sandwich. "This? I eat one every day. Why?"

Gary shrugged. "Just wondered if they were made today." He ignored Hugh's frown and picked up a banana and a carton of chocolate milk. He squinted at the expiration date. Five days from today. This would hold him until dinner.

He and Hugh stood in line and waited to pay. Hugh turned back around. "Busy this semester?"

Okay, so he didn't know. And obviously, there were still plenty of students who wanted to major in French. Not that there was anything wrong with French, Gary thought, but it wasn't German. Well, maybe Hugh had some contacts. He'd been around almost as long as Gary.

"Busy? No, not at all. The German Department is out at the end of the semester."

Hugh turned all the way around. "Are you kidding me? What do you mean? 'Out' as in done?"

"Not kidding, and yes, done. *Kaput*," Gary said, and used his finger to indicate Hugh should pay the cashier. He pulled a ten-dollar bill from his front pocket and thought he'd better start bringing food to work instead of buying it in the cafeteria. Three dollars for a banana and milk was ridiculous. After he tucked his change back in his pocket, he caught up with Hugh, who was waiting for him at a nearby table.

"I hadn't heard anything about this, Gary. When did you find out?"

"I found out yesterday from the provost. Well, what are they going to do? No one takes German anymore. They said it was for 'financial exigency.' Whatever." He peeled his banana and took a big bite. "So, the French Department is alive and well?"

Hugh lifted a shoulder. "As far as I know. I probably have a dozen more students than you do. Most of the language students take Arabic and Chinese. Some Russian. They want jobs after all of this." He bit into his sandwich and inspected it. It was quiet as he chewed and swallowed. "I'm planning to retire next June, anyway."

"Good for you. No, really, I'm glad. But I need to find a job, Hugh. I have to work."

"Let me poke around, talk to a few people.

Are you willing to relocate?"

Gary finished his milk and wiped his mouth. "If I had to. My wife likes it here, though. We both do. I just don't want to close the door on an opportunity."

Hugh nodded. "Okay, I'll keep that in mind."

"Thanks. Listen, here's my email address at home. I'll probably only have access here until final grades are in." He took a paper napkin and wrote on it, then slid it across the table to Hugh.

Hugh folded the napkin and slipped it into his pocket. "*Auf Wiedersehen*, Gary."

Gary tossed the banana peel and milk carton in the trash bin and walked back to his office. Once inside, he locked the door and pulled a notepad from a drawer. He logged back on to his computer and continued searching employment opportunities for German professors.

Chapter Four

Dani Berset met her parents at the train station in Geneva. Karl appraised his daughter and felt the sting of tears in his eyes. She was so damned beautiful, he thought. Tall like her mother, lean and leggy. No wonder she was so in demand. He hugged her hard and rested his palms against the sides of her head, searing the picture of her face into his mind.

"You're too thin," he said.

"Stop, Papa. Happy birthday." She rubbed her cheek against his.

"Dani, those boots. They're gorgeous," Ella said, checking out the brown leather boots that ended just above her daughter's knees.

"I wore them for a photo shoot, and they let me keep them. Mama, you can borrow them," she added with a wink. "Come on, follow me."

Karl and Ella trailed behind Dani, who turned heads as she strode through the station. Men of all ages stopped to stare at the stunning young woman.

"Her outfit alone cost a small fortune," Ella whispered to her husband. "I know designer clothes, and those are some of the best."

"She's doing well," Karl replied, smiling at Dani in front of him, clad in teal leather. Her long hair was knotted at the nape of her neck, a shiny twist of brown and dark blonde. When she turned to the side, he admired her perfect nose and full lower lip. He and Ella had created her, raised her, and let her go, to pursue a career in modeling and fashion. But she was still his girl. He'd hold on to her as long as he could.

They enjoyed an elegant meal of artichoke soup, roasted duck legs, a bottle of wine, and chocolate mousse. And when Dani picked up the check as if it were nothing, Ella tried to take it from her hand.

"Dani, let me do this," Ella said.

"Absolutely not! Papa's birthday, my treat." She pulled a gold credit card from her small alligator clutch and placed it inside the leatherette folder.

"You must be making an awful lot of money, dear," Ella whispered.

"Will you shut up about the money?" Karl banged his fist on the table, rattling glasses and dishes. Patrons at the neighboring tables turned their heads to stare. Ella and Dani both froze. Even Karl paused, aware that he'd gone too far with such an eruption.

"Sorry," he murmured. "Thank you, darling girl." Dani stared at her father, her black-rimmed eyes wide and fearful. Ella sat speechless by his side. The waiter scurried to the table and picked up the bill.

The train ride back to Lausanne was quiet. Karl tried to read a magazine, but he simply stared at the words on the page. He couldn't start a conversation with his wife about the scene he'd made in the restaurant. He wouldn't know what to say. The rhythm of the train caused her body to fall against his, but she quickly righted herself and moved closer to the mirrorlike window. There was nothing but blackness interspersed occasionally with soft dabs of light from the villages as the train sped through. The twitch, the forgetfulness, the outburst – something was wrong. As he thought back, Karl realized he'd been irritable and absent-minded for the past year. He always thought it was just stress at work, but now he wondered if it was attributable to something worse. His knowledge of medical conditions was very limited, but he would have to call the doctor tomorrow.

***

After Klara had dressed her husband for the ten-step walk next door to their apartment, they all said their good nights and Lucia closed the heavy door, turning the knob to secure the lock. The boys were in bed, sound asleep. Michel sat alone in the living room, nursing a glass of wine. She and Klara had washed and dried the dishes, and Lucia had only to set the coffeepot for the morning. She wiped her hands, thought about joining her husband with a glass of wine, and decided against it. Some of her friends thought a glass of wine each day while pregnant didn't do any harm, but it was just as simple to forego it.

She sat down heavily next to him. "Why, Michel, why did you ruin the evening with that announcement?"

He set his glass down slowly, resting it on a wooden coaster. "Why? Because Jean-Bernard wants a dog." Before Lucia could counter, he held up one hand, his palm nearly in her face. "Because if I don't take *this* job, I'll very likely lose the one I have. Because we have another child on the way, Lulu, and it's a good raise in salary. And because I wanted to tell you alone, but that was impossible."

She stared at her hands in her lap. Her voice was barely a whisper. "How could you leave your parents? How can I?"

He took her hands in his and brought them to his heart. "They'd come with us, Lulu. Of course they would come with us. *Amore*, this is a big offer. It's the best hotel in Geneva. And the company will help us, with the move, with selling the house. We'll either find a house just like this one, or one large enough to accommodate everyone. Maybe even a dog for Jean-Bernard." He looked deeply into her eyes. "I will provide for my family."

"You really think you would lose your job if you don't move?" Lucia's eyes were wide.

Michel dropped his chin. "The hotel was bought out by a Saudi company, very big. Monsieur Rosolen retires at the end of the month. Monsieur Almazi may have someone already lined up for the manager's job, and who knows what other changes they could make? Lulu, they think well of me, otherwise they would not have offered such a big promotion. They want me to go to Geneva to see the hotel."

"When? Soon?"

"Probably," he nodded. "I'm sorry, *cherie*, I know it's a lot to take in. And I don't want Mama to worry."

"Your mother worries about everything these days, you know."

***

Gary arrived home first, and started dinner. He didn't mind; it kept him occupied. He chopped up carrots, celery, and leeks and slid the pieces into a warmed skillet slick with olive oil. A couple of chicken breasts, already seared in the same pan, rested on a covered plate. Once the vegetables were cooked, he placed the chicken back in the skillet and added chicken stock and white wine.

He heard Bernie's key in the lock and twisted the peppermill over the mixture.

"Hi, babe," she called from the entryway. "Something smells good!"

"Ten minutes," he said. "Enough time for you to change, if you want."

She stopped long enough to kiss his neck before disappearing into their bedroom to change into a tee shirt and yoga pants. Gary popped English muffins into the four-slot toaster.

He sprinkled salt and oregano to the mixture, turned the vegetables, and grabbed the small pan of pine nuts he'd toasted in advance.

"I'll open the wine," she said, pulling a bottle from the refrigerator. "How was your day?"

"Let's talk about yours first," he said, assembling their dinner on plates and carrying them to the table.

Bernie poured wine and joined him. "Okay, mine was boring. Boring client, boring case." She grinned. "I'd love to sink my teeth into something juicy," she added, slicing into her chicken breast. "Like this!" She popped a piece of chicken in her mouth.

Gary took a long swig before speaking. "The college is eliminating the German Department," he said.

Bernie dropped her fork and stared at him. "What? When? Did they just tell you today?"

"I found out yesterday. I wanted to wait until I could find the right way to tell you. But there is no right way." He drained his glass and refilled it. "No one signs up to take German anymore, Bernie. I knew my class size was dwindling. I only have one course to teach this semester. But I didn't think they'd just let me go."

"But you're tenured, honey."

"Yep. And I can opt for 'retraining.' Bernie, I'm the only German professor left. Remember? Haller retired and Wurzer died. They were never replaced. So the university eliminates the Department, offers to retrain me, but they can still dismiss me because of financial hardship if they want. I could teach Arabic or Spanish, once I've learned it well enough to teach it, but that would take years. The college is hiring more adjuncts, more part-timers. It's cheaper for them." He attacked his chicken with vigor, hacking off a large slice.

"What are you thinking? Any ideas?"

Gary shrugged. "I've been looking online for other positions. But moving to Kansas doesn't sound too inviting, does it?"

"You've been job-hunting? Did you think you might want to include me in this search? I practice here in New York."

"You practice independently, Bernie. With no benefits. We need health insurance. You could practice law anywhere."

"Not true," she said, raking her hands through her hair. The coppery curls flew everywhere, and Gary thought she looked so sexy. She raised her voice. "Are you telling me you'd consider relocating without asking me what I think?"

"No, of course not." Sexy and angry, he said to himself.

"Well, it sure sounds like it," she said. She pushed her plate away and leaned back. "Gary, we're a team. We'll work this out, but we'll do it together. And I'm pissed off that you didn't tell me yesterday."

"I was trying to figure out what to do."

"We figure it out together, *that's* what we do." Bernie stood up. "I've got work to finish." She left Gary at the table. He pulled her plate toward him and ate what was left.

***

Karl Berset shivered as he dressed. He'd been to see three different doctors in the past two days, undergoing physical and neurological testing. They always made you wait, he thought. Why was their time so much more precious than anyone else's? I had to take a day and a half off from work. He looked at his watch.

What a wonderful evening with Dani last night, he recalled. His beautiful daughter, so successful, so happy. She'd insisted on picking up the check, and Karl performed calculations in his head. A bottle of Châteauneuf-du-Pape, three meals, salads, dessert, coffee, after-dinner drinks for Ella and Dani. She must have dropped close to a thousand francs last night. Doing better than her old man, that was for sure.

"Karl, sorry about the delay," the doctor said, entering the examination room. He held a clipboard in his hand. Karl frowned; he figured all the doctors used laptops these days. And this guy was young, too. His old doctor had retired a few months ago, and this kid had taken over. "I've asked your wife to join us in my office," he said. He avoided eye contact, Karl noticed. That wasn't a good sign.

He followed the doctor down a corridor to an office flooded with sunshine. Ella was already seated in one of two chairs opposite the doctor's desk, and Karl took her outstretched hand as he sat down. He glanced at three framed degrees on the far wall.

"So, I've been poked and pricked for two days now. What's wrong with me?" Karl pulled his shoulders back and pressed both feet to the floor.

"You're right, Karl, there was a lot of testing, and I appreciate your patience and cooperation." He finally raised his eyes. "I'll be direct with you. The results of those tests point to Huntington's."

Karl drew his hand away from Ella and shook his head. "What is this Huntington's?"

The doctor ran a palm over the top of his head. "Huntington's disease is inherited. It causes a progressive breakdown of nerve cells in the brain. It usually results in cognitive and psychiatric disorders." He waited for Karl and Ella to absorb the information.

"Hmm. That's not good." Karl turned to look at Ella, whose face was as pale as a pearl. He tried to process the words. *A breakdown of nerve cells in the brain.* He looked at the doctor. "You said it's inherited. So one of my parents passed it to me. But neither of them ever showed any signs of physical or mental decline." He thought of his mother, at eighty-seven, feisty and strong. "Although I didn't have much of a relationship with my father. He left us when I was eighteen, and died four years later."

"Do you recall how old he was when he died?"

Karl tugged at his upper lip with his bottom teeth. "Probably about fifty, maybe not quite fifty."

The doctor scribbled on a piece of paper before looking up. "The disease is caused by an inherited defect in a single gene, Karl. A parent with the Huntington's gene can pass along either a defective copy of the gene or a healthy copy. Each child has a fifty percent chance of inheriting the defective gene. Unfortunately, you were on the wrong side of the coin." He gave Karl a small smile and peered at his file. "And it was most likely from your father. Your mother is still living, and healthy, correct?" He glanced up as Karl nodded. "If your mother has not developed any symptoms, then the gene does not lie with her."

The doctor shuffled some papers on his desk. "So, all those tests confirmed the presence of the disease. The symptoms usually develop between the ages of thirty and fifty, and you're now sixty." He cut his eyes to Ella. "Huntington's can provoke depression, anxiety, sometimes uncharacteristic anger. Mrs. Berset, have you noticed any marked changes in Karl's behavior or mood over the past few months, or even years?"

Ella shifted before speaking. "I'm not sure what you mean exactly," she murmured.

"It's alright, Ella. Tell him." Karl stared out the window that was behind the doctor's head. Sunlight danced along a metal sculpture in the garden. "Tell him what a bastard I've been."

She reached into her purse and pulled out a tissue, dabbing at her eyes before speaking. "We had some difficulty a few years ago. And yes, he's been irritable lately. He was not always this way."

Karl raised his hand, as if pointing to the ceiling. "Five years ago we separated, after Ella learned that I'd fathered a child out of wedlock. It happened thirty years ago, and I had no idea the girl had become pregnant, but she came to see me and told me there is a child, and it is mine. After I confessed to Ella, we lived apart for a time, but for the past couple of years, we've worked things out." Karl glanced at his wife. "Of course, now you'd have good reason to leave me, dear."

Ella grasped his hand and held it tightly. "I'll never leave," she choked out.

A breakdown of nerve cells in the brain. Karl's shoulders dropped as if leaden weights had been placed on them. "So this means my children have a fifty percent chance of developing the disease, too," he said in a monotone. From the corner of his eye, he saw Ella's head drop, like a flower after a hard storm has passed.

"I'm afraid so," the doctor replied. "A genetic test can be administered to someone who has a family history of the disease. It's called predictive testing. But the result of the test doesn't indicate when disease onset will begin or what symptoms are likely to appear first. Some people choose to do the test because they find it more stressful not knowing. Others may want to take the test before they make a decision about having children. Obviously, there is stress when one knows they're facing a fatal disease. The tests are only performed after extensive consultation with a genetic counselor. But, Karl, yes, your children should know."

My children, Karl thought with dread. Paul, with an expectant wife. Yes, he must be told. There was another generation to consider. Beautiful, lively Dani. He could hardly bear to think about Dani and Huntington's in the same thought. And there was one more. His child with Bernadette Maguire.

Chapter Five

Ten days before Christmas, as he was preparing the final exam he'd give to his students the following day, Gary found a job posting online. The University of Innsbruck was looking for a visiting professor to teach American business English to students. He picked up the phone and called a colleague, an Austrian named Lorenz who taught in Maryland. Lorenz happened to know someone at the university, and promised to make a call on his behalf.

"Let me speak with my wife tonight," Gary said. "I'm quite sure she'll be open to the idea, but I do need to tell her first. Could you contact your friend tomorrow?"

"Sure thing, Gary," said Lorenz. "And I'm sorry about your job being eliminated. It's tough everywhere for us. Even here the class size is shrinking."

They hung up and Gary finished the final touches for the last exam he'd ever give at the university. His office was nearly bare, but he didn't feel sad. This potential opportunity in Innsbruck excited him, and he knew Bernadette would feel the same way. She'd welcome the chance to return to Europe, especially Innsbruck, so close to her beloved Switzerland. They could sublet the New York apartment, since the job in Innsbruck was only for a year. And it looked like the university would provide housing and a generous stipend. They'd be fine.

He hurried home, with just a quick stop at the deli for bagels, cream cheese, and lox. A simple supper, but one they both enjoyed. He entered the building's lobby and opened the mailbox. As he stepped into the apartment, he set the deli items on the counter and thumbed through the stack of envelopes and catalogues. One envelope stopped him cold. A letter addressed to Bernie with a return address from Lausanne. Karl Berset. *What the hell?*

He must have finally made contact with Michael, Gary said to himself. *Wonderful.* If he showed the letter to Bernie tonight, she'd be focused only on whatever Berset had to say in that letter, and Gary really needed to talk to her about the Innsbruck job. He put the letter in his laptop bag and zipped it shut.

***

"I'll be back on Thursday," Michel said, zipping his suitcase. "There's a dinner tonight with the bosses, meetings tomorrow, and a walk-through Thursday morning. Then I'll be on my way back home."

"Okay," said Lucia. "I hope everything goes

well. But I'll miss you. I have my appointment with Dr. Schmidt this morning." She stood on her toes to kiss him.

"You know I would go with you if I could, *amore*. I'll miss you, too. I called my mother while you were waking the boys. She has my number, and I told her she should call Papa's doctor if something comes up that she can't handle. And call me after you see the doctor. Give her my best."

"We'll be fine, Michel. I'll call you in the afternoon and leave a message. Hurry up now, or you'll miss your train. You look very handsome in your suit." She ran her hand down the fine wool of his jacket.

Michel slipped into his overcoat and took a last sip of coffee. Jean-Bernard was at school, but father and son had enjoyed a quiet breakfast together earlier. He gave his wife a long kiss and headed out the door. Lucia watched him walk up the road toward the train station and said a silent prayer that everything would work out. The idea of moving to Geneva was daunting, and she wasn't certain how helpful the new company would be in assisting them. Either way, it was essential that they find a suitable house.

Later that afternoon, she telephoned him and was surprised when he picked up. "Michel!"

He chuckled. "You are surprised to hear me answer my own phone, Lulu? We have a break before dinner. I'm in a very nice room here at the hotel. It's beautiful, very grand." He stood at the window and looked out over the lake, then he snapped his fingers. "Oh, Lulu, how was your appointment? Everything fine?"

"Yes, everything is fine, but I had a strange conversation with Dr. Schmidt. She asked about everyone, you and the boys, then she asked if you had received any news lately."

"How would she know about the job?" Michel asked.

"That's what I said. How did she know about the job? And she stopped, and we were both confused. She didn't know about the job at all, and when I asked her what she was referring to, she wouldn't look in my eye. But she wanted to know if you had received a letter from Bernadette. Michel, what's going on?"

Michel frowned. Bernadette? He corresponded with her a few times a year, usually a photo of the boys or news of Fribourg. "I don't understand, Lulu. I haven't heard from Bernadette since my birthday in May. That was six months ago. What else did Dr. Schmidt say?"

"That's just it, Michel. She stopped talking, just closed her mouth and smiled. She finished the examination and that was it."

"Okay. Don't worry about it, Lulu. I will contact Bernadette as soon as I have a chance. I'm sure everything is fine. See you soon, *amore*." He clicked off and turned toward the window again.

***

Karl drew Ella closer to him in bed. "I sent

the letter almost a week ago. But nothing in reply."

"You did the right thing, Karl," Ella said quietly. "Her child needs to know. She will do the right thing."

"Yes, you're right. Thank you for contacting Dr. Schmidt," he said. After that catastrophic mess with his old friend Henri Rutz five years ago, Karl couldn't bring himself to call the private investigator again. Besides, this was too important to wait around for Henri. He hadn't found the child last time. Ella contacted Hanna Schmidt, then taken the train to Fribourg to meet with her, and Dr. Schmidt confirmed to Ella that she had treated Bernadette Maguire thirty years ago. When Ella explained the circumstances surrounding Karl's urgent need to find his biological child, Hanna provided Bernadette's address in New York. She was adamant, however, that Karl contact Bernadette directly to find out more about the child.

"And Hanna was certain of the correct address for Bernadette, yes?" Karl questioned. He knew it wasn't easy for Ella to revisit the old wounds, the remembrance of Karl's infidelity so long ago. But she knew he had another child, a child with the former American student, and she agreed that this child, who was now fully grown, needed to be told about the disease and should have the option of taking the genetic test if he or she wanted.

Ella turned on her back. "If you don't hear from her, I'll ask Hanna for a telephone number.

We can't wait too long."

"I know," he said, feeling the now familiar twitch under his eye. He wasn't sleepy. "Do you mind if I turn on the light?" He reached for the switch.

"No, I can't sleep either," she said, raising herself up on one elbow.

In the soft bedroom light, they discussed their children. Paul lived for the moment, taking each day in stride. He might refuse to take the test. Even if they pushed him, Karl knew that Paul would decide for himself. Dani would want to know. She is fearless, Karl thought, and would stare down the possibility of a difficult future. But Karl couldn't imagine either Paul or Dani with this disease; it was too painful to keep in his thoughts. Perhaps there would be a cure before it had a chance to ravage either of them. He and Ella would talk to the children at Christmas. Meanwhile, Karl waited to hear back from Bernadette. "Perhaps my letter was too cryptic," he said to Ella.

Dear Bernadette – Please forgive me for writing this letter, but Dr. Hanna Schmidt provided me with your address. I would not write to you were it not very important. I need to contact your child. Our child. Please, Bernadette, either send the contact information to me, or provide him or her with my address and telephone number. It is quite urgent. Thank you. Karl Berset

He didn't think it appropriate, and Ella agreed, to tell Bernadette the reason in the letter.

She was not at risk, and it would be difficult to write it all out in a letter. But he hadn't heard back from her. If Hanna could provide him with a telephone number, he would try to call Bernadette tomorrow.

Ella turned to face him. "We have no choice but to endure this, Karl. I'll never leave your side, you must know that."

"Will you let me love you, my darling?" Karl brushed his hand across his wife's cheek and felt the wetness of her tears.

"Please," she whispered, pulling him onto her.

Chapter Six

Gary set the table and lit candles. He'd picked up an autumn bouquet of asters and mums in vibrant fall colors and set a glass vase in the center of the table. He opened a bottle of Pinot Grigio and set it to chill inside the refrigerator.

When he heard Bernie open the door, his stomach did a little flip, like it did six years earlier when he met her again after so much time apart.

"Hi, honey – oh, look at this! Candles and flowers!" She dropped her briefcase by the door and grinned. "Uh-oh, is it a special day I've forgotten?"

"Not at all," Gary said, pouring wine into two glasses and handing one to his wife. "I just thought we could use a relaxing dinner. I know I've been a little on edge, and I'm sorry."

"Was today the final exam?" She cocked her head, trying to remember.

"Tomorrow," he replied. "Tonight is bagels and lox." He raised his eyebrows to her.

"Great! I'll change my clothes and be right

back," she added, setting down her wineglass and heading into their bedroom to change.

Gary pulled a plate from the refrigerator and peeled off plastic wrap. He laid the glistening pink lox on the table, and added a bowl of softened cream cheese, a plate of sliced red onion and tiny green capers, and retrieved the lightly toasted bagels from the oven. They sat down to a comforting supper.

After light conversation about Bernie's day and their Christmas plans with his children, Gary cleared his throat. "I did find out about a job today."

She stopped eating. "Really? You didn't tell me the minute I walked through the door?"

"It's not around here," he said carefully.

The corners of her mouth twitched, but Gary couldn't detect a smile. "Are we going to Kansas? Honey, don't tease about this. Where is it?"

He licked his lips and took a breath. "The University of Innsbruck. It's a visiting professor position for a year." He held his breath.

"Innsbruck, Austria?" Her mouth opened. She looked at the piece of bagel in her hand and set it down on her plate. "Wow." She stared at the plate, then back at her husband. "Gary, how did you find out about it?"

He shrugged. "I've been looking every day. There isn't much out there, you know. Well, outside of Kansas. After I saw the posting, I called my friend Lorenz. He's from Austria originally, teaches at Loyola in Baltimore. He even knows someone at the university and said he'd vouch for me." Gary reached across the table and grasped Bernie's hand. "I'd have a good shot at it. If you think it would be something we could manage. A year in Innsbruck." He squeezed her hand.

Bernie blinked. "A year in Innsbruck," she echoed. "Wow. I wouldn't be able to practice, though." She slipped her hand away from his and picked up the bagel.

Gary nodded. "You couldn't practice law, but I bet you could teach an adult ed course or something. *Innsbruck*, Bernie. We'd have an apartment and a pretty decent stipend." His eyes held hers.

She bowed her head and said nothing. Gary tapped his fingers against his thighs. When she raised her face, she met his eyes and he knew. "Let's do it, Gary. Let's go to Innsbruck!"

He leaned over to lick a bit of cream cheese from her lip, and dinner was forgotten, as was the letter still hidden in his laptop bag.

***

Michel was treated like royalty from the moment he stepped through the entrance of the hotel. He had a posh suite, far more than he required. He and Lucia and the boys would have had plenty of space in the room. He met Almazi and McDonald for dinner that evening, and the service and food were both first-rate. The Hotel de la Rose was a fine hotel, he thought, but this place was far superior, and Michel hoped he was up to the challenge. It seemed that the two men sitting with him had no doubts.

"Well, if you'll excuse me, I have to leave," said Burt McDonald as the plates were cleared. He pushed back from the table. "I've got an early train to Rotterdam in the morning; gotta get my beauty sleep." He stood and wiped his palm on his jacket.

Michel rose and took the man's outstretched hand. It was warm and moist, and Michel wondered if the man perspired constantly. McDonald left the dining room and Michel turned to Almazi.

"My brother is in town, Michel," said Gamil Almazi as he lit a cigar and leaned back in his chair. "He divides his time mainly between Geneva and Berlin." Gamil's eyes were nearly black and they held Michel's like a magnet. "He would like for you to join him tonight."

"Is your brother also in the hotel business?" Michel hated cigars, even very expensive ones, but he wasn't going to say anything, of course.

Gamil smiled and stared at the cigar between his fingers. "No, he had no interest in this business." He looked up at Michel and smiled. "Go on, enjoy yourself tonight. We'll see you back here for breakfast."

Michel wanted nothing more than to retire to his room and call Lucia before it was too late. "Perhaps just for a short time then." He looked around. "Is he in the hotel?"

"I don't know. He probably wants to find a

jazz club. You like jazz music?"

"Sure," Michel stammered. "I don't listen to it much, but sure." He figured if Gamil's brother had invited him out to listen to music, he should go; after all, the job was not yet secure.

"Fine then." Gamil extinguished his cigar and stood. "He will telephone you in your room." He extended his hand. "I like you very much, Jean-Michel. You have excellent table manners."

Michel tried not to laugh at the odd remark and silently thanked his mother for instilling those manners in him when he was a boy. "I'll see you in the morning, sir."

Michel returned to his room and waited. He didn't know whether to stay dressed in his suit or change into more casual attire. *I guess I could ask Gamil's brother when he calls,* Michel thought. In the meantime, he pulled out his cell phone and placed a quick call home.

"Lulu? Did I wake you?"

"Just turned out the light, *amore*. Did you have a nice evening?" Her voice was sleepy.

"Very nice dinner, *cherie*." No need to tell her of the impending late-night plans. "I just wanted to say good night. See you soon. I love you."

"*Ti amo.*" She clicked off as his room phone rang. He picked up. "Yes?"

"Jean-Michel? This is Farid, Gamil's brother." Michel noted no accent; Farid spoke perfect English.

"Yes, hello. Gamil said you would be calling."

"So, you will come out with my friend and

me?"

"Yeah, sure. I'm wearing a suit. Should I change?"

"If you like, Jean-Michel. Maybe lose the tie," he added with a laugh. "Come to the lobby when you're ready. We're in the bar. Just look for two darkly handsome men."

Michel laughed and hung up the phone. He checked the time: just after nine. He hoped he'd be back in his room by midnight, especially with tomorrow's meeting starting at eight.

In the lobby, Michel spotted the two men immediately. He introduced himself to Farid, who introduced him to Ibrahim. Farid was slighter in build than his brother Gamil, and looked younger by about ten years. He was well-dressed, in dark gray slacks and a white shirt open at the neck. His friend Ibrahim, tall and slender, wore dark slacks as well, and his bald head gleamed in the lobby light. Michel shook hands with the two men.

"So I understand we're going to listen to some jazz?" Michel asked. The men exchanged a glance.

"Well, there's music, yes." Farid leaned toward Michel. "It's a private club I belong to. You are my guest this evening." Seeing Michel's surprised expression, he said, "Trust me, you will not be disappointed." His lip curled and he narrowed his eyes at Michel.

The three men climbed into a waiting car, and Farid spoke in Arabic to the driver, who nodded and sped away. Michel tried to steady his rapid heartbeat and vowed not to consume any alcohol. *I will not be disappointed*, he thought. *What did Farid mean by that?* He looked out the window and knew the lake was on his right. So we are heading toward Nyon.

They arrived at a tall, nondescript building. A giant of a man stood guard and waited while Farid pulled a card from his wallet. The guard looked at Farid, then at Ibrahim and finally at Michel. He nodded and stepped to the side to allow them access through the wide front door. Michel followed the two men to an elevator and the three of them stepped inside.

"Is this a strip club?" Michel had to know. Ibrahim seemed very focused on his fingernails.

Farid replied, "It's a private party." He bent his head closer to Michel as the elevator ascended. "You don't have to do anything you don't want to do. And if you choose to do...something, all expenses are covered, okay?" Michel had no idea what he was talking about. He looked up at the floor numbers, illuminating in succession above the elevator doors.

At the twenty-first floor, the doors opened and Farid led the way into a large room with damask-covered walls and heavy, sparkling chandeliers. All the people were beautiful, Michel thought, like movie stars, or models. "Follow me," Farid said, and Ibrahim and Michel walked behind him to the far side of the huge room. They took seats at a round table in a dimly-lit corner.

A waitress in a short, tight black dress approached, and Farid ordered a bottle of champagne and something called Veen, which turned out to be bottled water. Michel was unfamiliar with Veen, and had only sipped champagne once, at his wedding dinner. He looked around the room at people laughing, drinking, engaged in conversation. Like a normal cocktail party. A quartet played soft music on the other side of the room, and a few people were dancing.

"So, Jean-Michel, what do you think so far?" Farid leaned back in his chair, just as his brother had done earlier in the evening. Michel wondered if Farid also would light a cigar.

"It's very nice," Michel said, at a loss for words. "A beautiful room." Farid smiled at Ibrahim as the waitress returned with champagne and water.

"We invited a few friends to join us," Farid said. "There is someone in particular just for you," he added, his dark eyes heavy-lidded and unreadable. "If you would like some private time with her, there is a room upstairs." He slipped a key card from his pocket and slid it across the table to Michel. "You do not have to pay anything, understood? She is yours if you wish. No strings, no questions asked."

A prostitute! Oh shit, thought Michel. Was this a test for the new job? He assumed Farid was Muslim. Muslims and hookers together? No, that can't be, Michel told himself. Farid must not be Muslim. Oh man. He gulped water from a heavy crystal goblet.

Farid raised his hand in greeting and stood

up. Michel heard them before he saw them. High heels on a wooden floor. The jangle of bracelets. The swish of silk.

"Farid, my pet," one of them cooed as she crossed to him. He sat, and she perched on his lap, her face close to his. Her long hair curtained her face as she whispered to Farid. She was dressed in a creamy leather dress and thigh-high boots. Michel looked away and watched another woman drop into a chair next to Ibrahim, a waiflike blonde in a shiny black dress. Gold bracelets ringed her stick-like forearm.

"Well, hello there," he heard in his left ear and swiveled to look into the black-rimmed eyes of a beauty. Her full lower lip glistened dark pink and she smelled exotic, like a rare and very expensive spice. "I'm Dani, what's your name?"

Michel felt drops of sweat pop out on his neck and back. "Jean-Michel, nice to meet you," he croaked. He kept his left hand on the table so she'd see his wedding band, but realized this girl wouldn't care. She likely saw gold bands all the time. If this was such an exclusive party, Michel thought, these girls are very high-priced prostitutes. And Farid said she was paid for already, whether anything transpired between them or not, and of course, nothing would happen, Michel reminded himself.

Farid poured champagne into six tall flutes. So he drinks, too, Michel mused. The few Muslims he knew, from school and work, didn't drink, and most definitely didn't cavort with prostitutes. Farid made eye contact with Michel, and when he raised his eyebrows, Michel looked away.

***

Over breakfast, Gary and Bernie discussed the possibility of relocating to Innsbruck.

"Well, the position is for a year, with an option to stay if invited by the faculty," Gary said. He tore open a packet of sugar and poured it into his cup. "You like the idea, don't you, honey?" He stirred his coffee and raised the mug to his lips.

"I do," she replied. "It's exciting. As long as we can manage on your salary, yes, let's do it." Her eyes sparkled, and Gary knew she wanted to go. She'd be able to see Michael, and his children, too.

"Listen, I need to be at school," Gary said abruptly, swilling down the rest of his coffee and plucking a banana from a bowl in the middle of the table. "I have a couple of morning meetings and the final exam is at two. And I think they're throwing me a party," he added with a roll of his eyes. He unzipped his laptop bag to tuck the banana inside and stopped.

"Oh! Bernie, I forgot. This came for you in yesterday's mail. I put it in the bag and with all the news about the job, it completely slipped my mind." Little white lie, he told himself. She wouldn't know it arrived the day before yesterday. He handed the envelope to her. She stared at the return address and looked up at him. He glanced at the clock. Shit, he'd be late.

But he couldn't just walk out now.

Bernie slid her finger under the flap and opened the envelope. She unfolded one sheet of ivory white paper. As she scanned the sheet, her forehead worked up a little crease that Gary usually found adorable. She read aloud:

Dear Bernadette – Please forgive me for writing this letter, but Dr. Hanna Schmidt provided me with your address. I would not write to you were it not very important. I need to contact your child. Our child. Please, Bernadette, either send the contact information to me, or provide him or her with my address and telephone number. It is quite urgent. Thank you. Karl Berset

She stared at the letter. Gary made what he hoped was a light noise with his throat.

"Well, if he took the time to write to you, and asked Hanna for your address, it must be important," Gary said, edging toward the door. "Babe, I'm sorry, but I really need to go."

"Yeah, that's fine, go," she said in a distant voice. "He left a telephone number." She continued to stare at the letter.

"Bernie," Gary said sharply, causing her to jerk her head up and look at him. "Call him now." He blew a kiss to her and was gone.

***

Karl was in the office when his cell phone rang. The caller identification did not register a local number, but read "INTL" and Karl knew it would be Bernadette. He drew in a deep breath before touching the "answer" button on his phone.

"This is Karl Berset." He heard her own sharp intake of breath before she spoke.

"It's Bernadette."

"Yes, Bernadette, thank you for calling." Her voice sounded exactly the same and he closed his eyes.

"Your letter sounded urgent. I thought it best to call right away. Karl, what's going on?"

He knew he'd have to tell her about his disease, in order for her to give him the information he needed. Ella had tried to convince Hanna, but Dr. Schmidt was steadfast and would not divulge any clue about Bernadette's child. Karl swiveled in his chair and stared out the office window at a milky sky. "I have recently received a diagnosis. It's called Huntington's disease. It's, ah, not good, Bernadette. I don't know what you know about the disease, but it has already manifested itself, and that is how I found out from the doctor. It's genetic, apparently, and my children will be told. But our child, your child, ah, could be affected. And it's only right that he, or she knows. Because there is a chance. I'm sorry, Bernadette, to be rambling like this."

He waited. There was silence on the other end. Finally Bernie spoke.

"I'm sorry, Karl. Truly. I know very little about the disease, but you said it's genetic, so it's passed on them, to your children?" Her voice cracked at the end and Karl winced. This was as difficult as telling Ella, especially on a long-distance telephone conversation.

"Bernadetta," he began, calling her by the name he'd used so many years ago, "there is a fifty percent chance that one of my children carries the gene. There is a test, a genetic test that one can have, to determine if they will get the disease. If the child does not have the marker, as it is called, then they do not get this Huntington's, ever, nor do their children. Some choose not to have the test. My wife, of course, knows all about this, but we've decided to wait until Christmas to tell our children. They will have a difficult decision to make. Your child should have the information as well. It is really imperative that he, er, she knows."

"Of course," she breathed. Karl imagined Bernadette as she had looked five years ago, when she showed up on his doorstep with the news that he'd fathered a child with her. That was the beginning of so much trouble, with Ella, with that Greek girl who took his money. Henri had done all he could to find her, even offering to contact the authorities in Greece, but Karl had stopped him. The money didn't matter, after he'd lost Ella. His relationships with his children were fractured; he was out of his home. Thank God he had his Ella back with him now.

"The disease is progressing, Bernadette. Your child is now an adult, the same age as my son Paul. Please tell me, is it a young man? Or a young woman?"

"It's a him, Karl, a son. And you're right, he's a grown man now, nearly thirty years old. He's married, with children of his own. He has to know about this."

"He has children," Karl repeated, almost to himself. He slumped in his chair and watched snowflakes fall, fat white flakes floating through the air. One heavy cloud in the winter sky, filled with snow. Shades of white and gray outside; everything devoid of color.

"Karl, I will give you his contact information, but will you wait one day please, before you get in touch with him? Please let me speak with him first. He and I have remained close."

Karl needed to end the call. "Yes, of course I will wait." The words came out garbled. He wondered if she noticed.

She recited the address and Karl copied it down with a shaky hand. "He has an email address at the hotel," and she gave him that as well. "I'll call him today, Karl."

"Thank you, Bernadetta," he said, again letting slip the name he used to call her. "Goodbye."

"Karl," she said, stopping him before he could hang up. "Karl, I'm very sorry about this." He heard her sniffle on the other end and said "Thank you," once more time before ending the call.

Chapter Seven

Michel sat through meeting after meeting on Wednesday, taking notes. But he kept going over in his mind the previous evening, and the girl named Dani.

At the private club, he had agreed to go with Dani, if only to get away from the group at the table. They walked together to a private elevator and ascended one floor. Dani led him to a room down a long, quiet corridor. She touched a keypad and opened the door. They entered a room, like a hotel room, but with more personal touches, and Michel wondered if this was Dani's private apartment. She turned, standing just inches from him. She smiled, but her eyes were lifeless. It was as if she was operating on autopilot.

"Dani, is it? Dani, listen, nothing is going to happen in here, between us. I want you to know that right away. I'm a very happily married man." He held up his left hand. "I came out with these guys, I thought we were going to listen to some music. I hope you understand." There, he'd said it. Now he could leave.

She seemed to come out of her trance and blinked hard at him. "Really? It's Jean-Michel, yes?" He nodded. "Okay, Jean-Michel, but then why did you leave your table to come here with me?" She pushed out her lower lip into a pout, and Michel was sure that tiny gesture worked magic on her male 'guests.'

"It's called saving face, do you understand?" She shook her head. He pulled at his shirt collar and looked around the room. There was a bar at the other end and he headed to it. "Do you want something?"

"Whatever you're having," she murmured, shrugging off her jacket.

"I'm having water," he said pointedly, to which she simply nodded. He pulled two bottles from the small refrigerator. "Do you want a glass?" She shook her head and he brought two bottles over to the sofa, where she sat. He lowered himself to the soft cushion and handed her a bottle.

"Saving face means preserving dignity, honor. You know this man Farid? He is brother to the man I will most likely be working for soon. I didn't want to insult him." Michel shook his head and gulped down water. "I need this new job, but I don't know these people at all."

Dani laid her hand on his thigh. "What do you want to do then? I can do everything else. You can just watch if you want." Her eyes were wide, like a child's, and Michel thought she couldn't be much older than twenty.

He took her hand in his and moved it off his

leg. "I want to drink this water, and then I'm going to take a taxi back to the hotel. And if you would be so kind as to not say anything about what did or didn't happen in here, I'd be grateful."

"I never talk about anything," Dani said, frowning.

"Are you paid well?"

She laughed, tossing her head back, her hair shimmering in the soft light of the room. "Very, very well, thank you."

"Okay, good then. As long as you're happy," he said, not looking at her. He couldn't imagine that she was happy, but what did he know? He was just a small-town boy in the big city. As long as Gamil hadn't set him up. That was the one thing that gnawed at the back of his mind. If this was a requirement for getting the job, he didn't want it. He had an excellent career record, and he'd find another job if the hotel decided not to hire him. Michel finished his bottle of water and stood up.

"Dani," he said, extending his hand. She took it and rose to her feet. "It was nice to meet you. But please don't be offended when I say I hope I never meet you again."

She grinned. "This was the first time I ever brought a man here to drink water."

He found the hotel card Farid had given him earlier and handed it to Dani. "You can throw this away for all I care. I don't know what room it's for, but I don't need it. You take care of yourself," he said before letting himself out of the room.

In a taxi on the way back to his hotel, Michel checked his phone. There was a voice message from Bernadette. "Michael, hi, it's me. Listen, we need to talk, soon. As soon as possible, please. I'm okay, nothing's wrong, but call me when you get this message. It doesn't matter what time it is. Just call me please. Thanks." Michel checked his watch. It was nearly one, so it would only be early evening in New York. He punched in her number and waited for the call to connect.

"Bernadette, *salut*. I hope this isn't a bad time," Michel said when Bernie picked up.

"Sweetheart, listen to me. This is really important. Your father, not Bruno, your birth father, contacted me. We spoke earlier today. You need to speak with him as soon as possible."

"What? Why? There is no reason. I don't understand."

"There is reason, Michael. He's sick. He has a disease, and it's bad. I don't know how long he'll live with it. I don't know much about it, but as the disease progresses, it will be harder for him to communicate."

"Does he have cancer?"

"No, it's called Huntington's Disease. It destroys nerve cells in the brain. And it's genetic."

"What do you mean?"

"It's inherited, honey. It's in the genes. And that means there's a chance you could have it, and if you have it, your children could have it as well."

Michel couldn't breathe. "*What?*" His throat felt like sandpaper, like that time after he'd screamed at a rugby game. "My children? Bernadette, I don't understand any of this." The taxi moved along quickly, skirting Lake Geneva, making its way back to the hotel. There was no traffic at this late hour.

"Michael, darling, listen carefully. He wants to write to you, or email you. I didn't give him your phone number."

"No. No writing, no emailing. Where is he? I will see him. I want to see him. We must speak about this."

Bernie sighed. "Okay, here is his address. Write it down."

"Wait. Please. Hold on, I'm in a taxi." He pulled a business card from his wallet and asked the driver for a pen. "Okay."

Bernie recited Karl's address in Lausanne and waited. "And here is his telephone number."

"My children. Lucia is pregnant." He was traveling through blackness.

"Michael, sweetheart, listen. You may not be carrying the gene, okay? Fifty percent chance you *don't* have it. And if you don't have it, your children will never have it. But you need to know. I told Karl not to contact you until I had a chance to speak with you first. I know you didn't want to know this man, I realize that, and I thought you'd never need to meet him. He's not well, Michael. I don't hate him, and I don't want you to hate him, either."

"I'm sorry, Bernadette. I hate him very

much right now. Thank you for the information. I have to go." He clicked off as the taxi stopped in front of the hotel. He gave the driver his pen and money for the ride, and slammed the door behind him.

He ran to the elevator and as soon as the doors closed, he fell against the wall, trying to fill his empty lungs with oxygen. *A genetic disease? I might have passed to my children?* The doors parted and he ran down the corridor. When he finally reached his room, he fumbled for the card to open the door. After jamming the card in the slot, he took a breath and tried once again. The lock gave way and he burst into the room, falling to his knees on the carpet, heaving great breaths. *I could have a disease. My children could have it as well.* He threw his phone across the room, but it landed on the bed and didn't break, although at the moment he didn't much care if it smashed into pieces. There would be no sleep; that much he knew for sure. He left his clothes in a pile on the floor and crawled into a bed that was far too big for one person.

Michel snapped back to the present and knew what he had to do.

***

Ella thought Karl should tell his mother, but he had his doubts.

"She's eighty-seven, Ella. She doesn't need to hear this news. It will upset her," he said.

"She may outlive you," Ella said. "She should

know."

"It will be too much for her to take in," Karl replied.

Their discussion was interrupted by a knock on the front door. Ella opened it to see a young police officer. With a somber face and his hat in hand, he asked for Karl Berset.

"Bring him in, Ella, please," Karl called from the chair.

Ella escorted the officer into their living room and invited him to sit, but the man declined. Standing as straight as an arrow, he informed Karl that Mathilde Berset was found dead in her apartment that morning. One of her neighbors had called the police when Mathilde didn't show up for the Wednesday morning coffee group. It appeared she'd died of natural causes, most likely the previous evening.

Karl peered at the police officer, then bowed his head and absorbed the unexpected news. Just a week before Christmas, too. His mother did love Christmas - the lights, the carols, the anticipation. But she lived to eighty-seven, and that was quite a life. With the slightest pang of guilt, he thought about the bank account in her name, money that surely would be appreciated now, especially if he had to retire early from his job. He knew his mother had nearly a million Swiss francs to her name. He lifted his chin and spoke to the officer.

"Thank you very much for the information. We will go to her. Where is the body now?"

"She's at the hospital. If you would like to

come with me, I'll take you to the registry office. You'll need to confirm the identity before the office can issue a death certificate."

"Of course," Karl said. He tried to remember his mother's birthday, and couldn't. The doctor's prognosis rang in his head – *has the disease attacked my brain already?* He turned to Ella in panic. "I think I'm losing my mind," he whispered.

Ella turned to the officer. "We'll follow you in our car," she said. "Thank you again, and we'll just be a few minutes." She walked with the officer to the door and closed it, then hurried back to Karl, who sat motionless, staring with unfocused eyes at nothing. She knelt before him and laid her hand against his cheek.

"Karl, dear, listen. This is quite a shock. You are not losing your mind, do you understand?" Her voice was unusually sharp, Karl thought, and he turned his focus to her. "Your mother passed away peacefully, and that is a blessing. To live to the age of eighty-seven, that is also a blessing. So come on, let's go to the hospital. I'll drive." She stood up and held her hands out. Karl rose from his chair, slowly, as if he, too, were eighty-seven years old.

He snapped his fingers. "Of course, August first. Swiss independence day."

Ella peered at him. "Your mother's birthday. Yes, Karl. Come now."

The doorbell rang again and Karl snapped. "We said five minutes! My God, could he leave us alone!" His swift outburst caught him by surprise. "Sorry," he muttered in Ella's direction.

Ella used her hand to signal calm and opened the door, expecting to find the police officer waiting. "Oh," she said. "May I help you?"

Michel extended his hand. "I'm Jean-Michel Eicher. I'm here to speak with Karl Berset."

Chapter Eight

"I have an online interview with them tomorrow," Gary said over coffee. "I guess I should hold off buying tickets until then, right?"

Bernie nodded. "I'm sure you'll get the job, Gary, but the tickets will be expensive with short notice. Do you think they'll let you know today?"

"Lorenz said it's just a formality. I emailed my credentials to them, they have access to all the articles I've published. They know I'm fluent."

"You going to tell the kids before Christmas, or spring it on them when they show up?" Her eyes teased him. "You think Nicky will be okay with this?"

"She'll be fine. She's so healthy, so centered now. She was telling me about her spring break plans last week. Hey, I saw that face. Really, Bernie they'll be fine. Something else bothering you, sweetheart?"

Bernie sighed. "That letter from Karl Berset? He's sick, Gary. He has Huntington's disease."

Gary looked up. "Huntington's? Isn't that

like Parkinson's?"

Bernie shook her head. "Not the same. Huntington's affects personality. It's pretty bad. I don't know how fast it progresses, but he's had symptoms already, which is how he found out." She laid her hand on Gary's. "More importantly, the disease is inherited. A child of a parent with Huntington's has a fifty-fifty chance of getting it."

"Oh God, Bernie." Gary understood what she meant. "Michael knows?"

"I called him yesterday after I spoke with Karl. It's devastating. Michael's very angry, of course. He's never even met Karl, and he hates him. I think I was able to convince him to contact Karl. I know he never wanted to have a relationship with him, but I'm hoping that once he talks with Lucia, he'll realize how important it is to be informed. He can be tested, you know, to find out if he's carrying the gene for the disease."

"What good would that do? And why would he want to know?"

Bernie shrugged. "You wouldn't want to know? He's got kids. If he has the gene, it means he'll get the disease, and the fifty-fifty chance is passed on to his kids." She looked away from Gary. "Maybe there'd be a cure by then."

"Karl also has children, right?" Bernie nodded again. "Wow. Well, I'm sorry. Even for him."

"Yeah, me, too. And especially for my Michael." She looked at Gary with shiny eyes.

***

Karl rose on unsteady legs and walked to the door as Ella stepped away. He pulled his right hand from his pocket and offered it, quivering, to Michel. Michel gripped the man's hand, steadying its tremor. Karl stared at him, seeing young Bernadette in his hair, his mouth, his cheekbones. But he has my brown eyes, Karl thought.

"I'm Jean-Michel Eicher," Michel said in a clear, strong voice. He withdrew his hand from Karl's and it dropped to his side.

"Karl Berset. I suppose I shouldn't be surprised that you're here. And it's good to finally meet you. Please come in, have a seat." Karl's eyes flitted to Ella, who nodded her approval. "This is my wife, Ella." Michel, still standing, shook hands with Karl's wife.

"Give me your coat, please," said Ella. "Would you like coffee? Tea? Water?"

"Nothing, thank you. I'm actually traveling back to Fribourg, but Bernadette telephoned me yesterday, so I stopped on my way home." Michel shifted his weight. His eyes traveled to Karl, and their glances met like crossed swords.

"Please, sit." Karl waved his hand toward the sofa. "I spoke with Bernadette yesterday as well." Karl eased himself into his chair and studied Michel. "You're a good-looking young man. Obviously, you got that from your mother."

"I really can't stay long," Michel said.

"Look, I just found out about this disease," Karl said, turning his palms up as if he were a street beggar asking for coins. He looked to Ella for confirmation.

"Jean-Michel, we were stunned," Ella said. "Until last month, we thought everything was normal. But Karl has had some memory lapses and he seemed out of sorts, perhaps more irritable."

"More irritable than usual," Karl interjected. "I didn't make too much of it, actually, but I knew I needed to see a doctor anyway, so I brought up the incidents and he had me tested."

"As soon as we learned of the diagnosis, Karl contacted Bernadette."

"You have children, I understand," Karl said, with nervous solicitude.

"My wife and I have two boys," Michel replied. "And another baby on the way. In the summer," he added, raising a hand to his chin, partially covering his mouth. He cleared his throat. "I have a fifty percent chance of developing this disease, is that correct?"

"Yes." Karl bit back the emotion that threatened to engulf him. "You can take a test to find out," he said. "Find out if you have the gene." *Which of my children will have the defective gene*, he wondered.

Ella brought water in from the kitchen. A pitcher, three plastic tumblers. "We've had our share of broken glass around here," she said with a small smile. She poured water, half a tumbler for Karl and handed it to him. His shaky hand brought the glass to his lips and he drank, spilling only a small amount before setting it back down.

She handed one to Michel. "If you decide to take the test, there is counseling available. If you do not have the gene for Huntington's, it means your children will never get it. If the test reveals that you have the gene, you will eventually get the disease, maybe not for a long time. And your children would have the fifty percent chance of developing it. And who knows, Jean-Michel, what medical science will be in the future. Perhaps a cure will exist by then." She touched his arm. "I know that doesn't ease the anxiety."

"No," Jean-Michel said, setting his plastic tumbler of water back on the table. "No, but I would want to know either way. I want to be tested." He met Karl's gaze. "I need to know, for my family's sake."

"I understand," Karl said.

"Well, I should go." Michel stood. "My wife is expecting me home today. I've been in Geneva since Tuesday."

"My daughter lives in Geneva."

"Will she be tested?"

Karl dropped his chin. "We haven't told the children yet. Next week, at Christmas, and then they can decide."

"I see," Michel murmured. "Well." He turned to Ella, who retrieved his coat.

Karl struggled to stand, but Michel raised his palm. "Please, don't get up. It's okay." Karl gripped Michel's outstretched hand.

"I'm sorry," he said, a crack running through his voice. "About everything."

Michel averted his eyes, away from Karl's face. "I know," he said, and walked to the door. He shook Ella's hand and was gone.

***

As the train from Lausanne sped north, Michel gazed out the window at the fallow fields, the vineyards bereft of fruit. One week to Christmas and he struggled to find any speck of holiday spirit.

I could be carrying a gene in my DNA that will one day render me useless. His father was slipping away, into the black waters of Alzheimer's. His mother had aged twenty years in the past six months, but was determined not to put her husband in a home for demented patients. He was about to lose his job at the Hotel de la Rose and start a new job, one that paid nearly double what he was earning but would have triple the responsibilities. And a new baby on the way. He rolled his shoulders.

Michel hadn't seen Farid since Tuesday night at the club. Gamil said nothing to him on Wednesday, so Michel didn't know whether he'd spoken with Farid. Perhaps Farid would tell his brother that Michel took up with one of the high-priced call girls. And perhaps Gamil would try to blackmail him with that piece of information, even if it wasn't true. Very likely Gamil also belonged to this club.

And Dani. Such a pretty girl, and young. So young to be involved in that business, but that's what the older men wanted. A girl young enough to be their daughter. In that profession, a girl's time was limited.

He opened a newspaper and read the same sentence five times before raising his eyes to look out the window again. Dani wasn't his problem. She was an adult, and she made her choices. There were plenty of other options for employment, and she obviously was comfortable with her decision. Michel couldn't wait to return to his Lucia, to his boys. Yes, there would be a serious talk ahead, and it pained him to think of telling Lucia the news about Karl Berset. She didn't need the worry right now. Neither did his parents. Perhaps there was no need to say anything yet. He closed his eyes.

It was good to speak with Bernadette again, even if the reason for her call was not. He was glad to hear her voice, her American accent. They usually exchanged emails every few months, and he was grateful to continue the relationship with her. Lucia loved Bernadette as well, but Michel usually didn't speak of her in front of his mother. Klara had enough to worry about with Bruno; Michel didn't want her thinking he favored Bernadette over her.

He opened his eyes and sighed heavily, drawing the attention of a young woman sitting opposite him. Their eyes met and she smiled shyly, then glanced down and saw the gold band on his finger. She reddened and turned away. He closed his eyes again until the train pulled into the station, then waited for everyone to exit before he stood. He reached and pulled his bag from the overhead rack, and stepped onto the platform.

Chapter Nine

Gary closed his laptop and sat still for a moment. Then he rocketed out of his chair and danced around the empty apartment. "Innsbruck!" he shouted to no one. He picked up his phone and typed one word to Bernie: *Pack!*

He waited for the phone to ring. As soon as she saw the text, he knew she'd call. And he waited. Okay, he thought, she's busy. She can't talk right now. He poured a glass of orange juice, gulped it down, washed the glass and set it upside-down on the drying rack.

"Come on, honey, call," he said to the phone. He spun it on the table. He tapped his fingers. Finally, he picked it up and dialed her number. And it went directly to voice mail.

"Babe, sorry to bother you. But call me when you get this. I got the job! I'll make the flight reservations as soon as I hear from you. Love."

Gary couldn't stay still. Too much nervous energy, he figured. He decided to clean the bathroom. That would make the phone ring. He changed the sheets, dusted the lampshades. Did thirty push-ups.

An hour later, Bernie still hadn't called back. He tried to remember what she'd said she had to do today. I should be a better listener, he thought. Was she in court? Probably. She might be there for hours. Maybe he should head uptown and meet her for lunch. Yes, take her to lunch. He'd stop in at her office, and if she wasn't there, he'd just go to the courthouse a few doors down.

He took a shower in the clean bathroom and dressed in the slacks she liked. He found a dark green sweater on a shelf in the closet and pulled it on over his tee shirt. Just before he headed out the door, he grabbed his leather jacket from the coat tree and hurried out to meet his wife.

***

Michel called in sick to work. In all the years he'd been employed at the hotel, he'd only called in twice, and that was at Lucia's insistence. Monsieur Rosolen told him not to worry about it and asked how everything went in Geneva.

"Fine, fine," Michel replied in a voice he tried to make sound hoarse and scratchy. "They're very nice people, and I think it will be a rather easy adjustment," he lied. Monsieur Rosolen cared, he knew, but he was also now quite wealthy after the buyout, and he planned to retire in Ascona, where his family had property. Next week would be his last at the hotel.

"Good, Michel. Well, you take care of yourself and we'll see you next week." There hadn't been a Christmas party for the past three years; instead, all the employees received a bonus in their paychecks, which was what everyone wanted anyway. "Get some rest."

Michel replaced the telephone in its cradle and lay back in bed. Lucia knew he wasn't really sick, and he had no intention of staying in bed all day pretending to be ill. He'd get up and help around the house, and assist his mother. Getting his father into the shower had become harder, as Bruno now seemed to have a fear of water. He made a mental note to speak to his mother about hiring a male nurse to help out, maybe an hour a day or so.

He heard Lucia singing to Luca, a song she must have sung as a little girl in Italy. Jean-Bernard had left for school already, walking the short distance up the road to join the other children. Everyone was excited about Christmas. Perhaps if he got out of bed now, he could help his mother before noon. Then, when little Luca took his nap, he'd have some time with Lucia.

Michel threw back the covers and swung his legs around to the floor. He made the bed, knowing Lucia would appreciate the gesture. Then he took a quick shower and dressed for the day.

"Breakfast, *amore*?" She held a sleepy Luca in her lap. At three, he was really a Mama's boy, so clingy, thought Michel. He tousled his boy's thick dark hair, eliciting a gummy grin.

"I'll get it, *cherie*. What about you? Some fruit? Muesli?"

"Sure. Luca, you sit in your big boy chair while Mama and Papa eat." She strapped him in and put a small handful of cereal flakes on the tray in front of him.

Michel placed a container of yogurt, a box of Muesli, and two bowls and spoons on the table. He spooned yogurt into the bowls and poured some Muesli on top of each, then slid one of the bowls to his wife. "Oh, the honey," he said, getting up to retrieve the small jar from the cupboard. He squeezed a drizzle on her bowl first, then his own.

"So, you like the hotel? And the city?" Lucia chewed her lip while she mixed her cereal.

"Lulu." Michel glanced at his son, who was happily playing with his cereal flakes. His throat tightened as he watched him, happy, carefree. He pressed his lips together and tried to fight the pressure building behind his eyes.

"Michel, what is it?" Lucia stopped stirring and grasped his hand. "They took away the job?"

He shook his head. "Lulu, Bernadette called while I was in Geneva. The man who fathered me is named Karl Berset. He lives in Lausanne with his family. He's very sick. He has a disease. A genetic disease that is passed down from a parent to a child." She gasped and gripped his hand more tightly.

"Michel..." Her lips moved but no other words came from her mouth.

"He contacted Dr. Schmidt first, to try and

find Bernadette. He knew she had delivered me. That is why Dr. Schmidt asked you those questions, because she already knew."

"She should have explained," said Lucia.

"I'm sure she didn't want to be the person who spilled the news. But she gave Karl Berset an address for Bernadette in New York, and he contacted her because he knew I existed. So Bernadette called me and told me the awful news, and I asked her for his address in Lausanne. Yesterday I went to his house. After I left the hotel, I stopped in Lausanne." His eyes searched hers for something to hold on to.

"I met him, Lulu. He looks normal, but he told me he has twitches sometimes, and his wife said his mood can be unpredictable." He stopped for air. It was as if his lungs were contracting and he took gulps, big gulps of air. It wasn't so much the idea of Karl Berset's disease, or even his mortality. He'd only just met the man who'd fathered him. What shook him was the idea that he could be carrying the deadly gene and may have passed it on to his sons, and to the tiny one living in Lucia's belly.

"There is a test. I can take it if we choose. It will let me know if I have the gene that brings the disease. Fifty-fifty chance." He stared hard at the table, then lifted his eyes to Luca, little Luca, who beamed up at him. "I want to know, *cherie*. I need to know. For our children."

"The children." She laid both hands on her stomach, guarding the precious life inside.

He swallowed again. "If I don't have the

gene, the children will never get the disease."

"But if you do – oh, Michel," she said, and her pretty face crumpled into tears.

"Mama?" Luca turned his big brown eyes to his mother. His lower lip trembled.

"Oh, Luca, my darling boy," Lucia whispered, pulling him to her lap and stroking his hair, even as tears fell.

"I'm so sorry, Lulu," Michel choked. "Let me hold him, please."

Lucia turned in her chair to face Michel, who took the boy in his arms and rocked him from side to side. Luca stuck his tiny thumb in his mouth and pressed his cheek against Michel's chest.

"What is this disease called?" Lucia asked in a hoarse whisper.

"Huntington's." Michel rested his cheek on top of Luca's head. "And because of this disease, I have now met the man who fathered me." He thought about Karl Berset, his face, his voice, and wondered if he resembled him at all.

"Do you hate him?"

"I did at first. After Bernadette's call, I hated him so much. But I don't now, Lulu. He is an old, broken man. Facing a certain death, and a terrible journey to the end." He paused, and pulled his son closer. "I was very sad to leave, realizing I'd never known him."

"And what about his wife?"

"Ella," Michel said. "Very nice. They have children, a son and a daughter. Karl said he'll tell them about his illness at Christmas."

"So very sad," she murmured. "Sometimes we think our problems are the only problems in the world. But people we don't even know have struggles, some of them much more difficult than ours."

"Yes." Michel stood and brought the sleeping Luca to the sofa in the living room. He turned to his wife. "I want to hire a nurse for Papa, a male nurse if possible. It's becoming too much for Mama to handle, and you, you have the boys and you need to take care of yourself. Someone to help with bathing and feeding, until we move, and then we find someone else. I hope Mama will let me. And Lucia, not a word about Karl or the disease to Mama, please."

"No, of course not, *amore*."

They returned to the kitchen and both finished their cereal standing up. Lucia took the empty bowls to the sink. "She'll be surprised to see you home."

"I know. Let's not say I called in sick. Just a vacation day." He picked up a towel to dry the bowls she'd just washed.

"When do you think we will move to Geneva?"

Michel sighed. He had the job, he knew that much, but he needed to contact Gamil about the move and housing. "Soon, Lulu. I will call to find out the exact day." He put the bowls back in the cupboard and wondered when Gamil would telephone. "I'll stop in next door to say hello. You stay here and sleep while Luca naps. Take him in the bed with you." He bent to kiss his wife. "I'll be back."

***

Still reeling from Jean-Michel's visit, Karl was faced with the task of identifying his dead mother at the hospital. But he couldn't move.

He stared into space, thinking about Jean-Michel, his son. Bernadette's boy, who looked so much like her. A grown man, the same age as his Paul, and yet, so very different. Both men created by me, Karl thought. Two sons. I have two sons.

"The boy looks like you, Karl," Ella said in a soft voice behind him. "He is a fine young man."

Karl extended his hand, and when she took it, he pulled her down to sit on the chair's wide arm. "Do you think he'll test?"

"With children of his own, yes, I think he will. I can't imagine Paul and Dani wouldn't want to know, too." She ran her fingertips through his hair.

"Maybe we should tell them before Christmas, *cherie*." Karl's eyes asked for confirmation. "Better than saving bad news for a day that should be celebrated."

"Whatever you say. But we have to go to the hospital now." She stood up and offered her hand. "I'll drive."

On the way to the hospital, Karl telephoned the family's lawyer. After expressing his condolences on Mathilde's passing, the attorney said, "Your name is on all her accounts, Karl, which is good. You can access her money to pay expenses. And, of course, everything she had goes directly to you. You are the sole beneficiary."

"Yes, okay. I'll call you back when the arrangements are set." He disconnected the call and slipped the small phone into his jacket pocket. His mother had always been adamant about not having a funeral. *'Just take my ashes and scatter them in the Parc de la Gottettaz,'* she'd said on frequent occasions. He was bound to honor her wishes.

It didn't take long to identify the body. Karl looked into the serene face of his aged mother and nodded. She looked peaceful and rested, and Karl touched his fingers to her cheek in a final gesture. *Bonne nuit, Mama,* he thought. Sleep in peace.

There were forms to fill out, which Ella handled, as Karl didn't trust his hand and fingers to work properly. Once the paperwork was done, they walked arm in arm out of the hospital. Karl stopped to stand in the sunlight.

"She spared me the task of having to tell her," he said quietly. "She never knew about my father – he left us and died too soon." Karl turned his face to the sky, letting the weak winter sun touch his face before getting into the car.

"Why didn't your mother keep her accounts at your bank, I wonder," Ella said, maneuvering through light traffic.

"She said she wanted her independence," Karl replied with a hard laugh. "She didn't realize I could have accessed her accounts at any time.

My name is on everything she owned." He sighed. "I wish I'd had the chance to say goodbye, though."

"I know, my love. You'll have to speak to her spirit," Ella said as she turned onto their street. "We can always spend time in the park and visit her." Karl laughed out loud at her remark.

The following day, at Mathilde's bank, Karl forgot why they were there, but wouldn't admit it to Ella. She found a chair for him and stood, waiting to speak with a representative. When an employee approached, Ella took charge and asked for some privacy.

The woman led Karl and Ella to an office at the back of the bank, and closed the door after she'd gestured at two chairs across from her desk. She waited, and when Karl stared at her blankly, Ella spoke.

"My husband's mother has died," Ella began. "Mathilde Berset. I have the certificate." As Ella opened her purse to retrieve the death certificate, Karl remembered.

"My name is on all of her accounts, and I may need to access some of the funds there." He beamed at Ella.

The young woman glanced at the death certificate and began typing on her computer keyboard. She frowned, typed some more, and raised her head to look at the couple seated across from her.

"Your mother's account is nearly at zero, Monsieur. There is a total of three hundred sixty-four francs in the account. Many withdrawals," she added, squinting at her computer screen. "Many."

"*What?*" Karl started to rise, only to be held down by his wife. "What are you talking about? My mother had nearly a million francs in her account." He pushed the soles of his feet to the floor.

The woman looked away from her computer screen and removed her glasses. "Yes, Monsieur Berset, she did have nearly nine hundred thousand Swiss francs about eighteen months ago. Let me print out this statement for you." She typed again and the printer behind her desk began to spit out paper. She swiveled around in her chair and pulled the papers from the printer. Then she laid them on the desk, so they were facing Karl and Ella. With her pencil, she pointed out the withdrawals, one every few days, for thousands of francs each time. Over the course of a year and a half, Mathilde Berset had withdrawn well over eight hundred thousand Swiss francs. She was nearly penniless when she died.

Karl's face contorted as he stared at the bank statement. He knew his rage was about to spill over, but he couldn't do anything to stop it. He started pounding both fists on the desk, until Ella stood and grasped his hands.

"My husband is not well," she said to the bank employee. "Karl, let's go," she whispered loudly to her husband.

"Where is her money?" he shouted, drawing the attention of people outside the closed office door. When he stood, his legs gave way, and he crumpled to the floor, sobbing like a little boy.

Chapter Ten

Michel was exhausted. He'd stayed up past midnight, unable to settle his brain. Lucia was still in bed, snoring lightly. He stuck his head in the boys' room, and his heart seized at the sight of their perfect little faces. Jean-Bernard clutched a worn brown stuffed horse, one he'd had since he was a baby and refused to give up at bedtime. Luca's thumb was in his mouth, his tiny body curled on its side.

The presents were all assembled and under the tree. He'd set the timer on the coffeepot, and even checked in next door to ensure his parents were settled. Klara had finally agreed to give Bruno medication that would help him sleep through the night, which meant she could sleep, too.

They were moving in four days, as Gamil wanted Michel to start the new job on the Monday following New Year's Day. So much to do, and not enough time, Michel thought. He poured a small glass of brandy and lifted his sock-clad feet to the table in front of the sofa. His first counseling session, a kind of pre-test, was scheduled for January 9, a Friday, and Lucia insisted he not reschedule, in spite of the move and the new job. However, he conveyed to the counseling office that he could only take appointments in the evenings or on weekends, and if he was needed at work, he would have to cancel or reschedule. His physician wanted Michel to have at least three appointments with the genetic counselor before undergoing the test. Michel just wanted to know whether he carried the gene or not.

He finished the brandy and stretched out on the couch. Within minutes, he was fast asleep.

***

Gary's children would arrive soon, to spend Christmas day and night in the apartment. Bernie was busy cleaning, and Gary had gone out to buy food, knowing what Justin and Nicole preferred. Gifts for the kids were small - Gary said they'd be happiest with cash or gift cards. She arranged the flat little packages around their tabletop Christmas tree. The kids would return to Connecticut the next afternoon to spend the rest of Christmas break with their mom and her husband. And Bernie still had packing to do.

Gary returned with two cloth shopping bags and Bernie laughed as he unpacked a bag of potato chips, sour cream and onion dip, chicken wings.

"Is all of that for Justin?" She unpacked the other shopping bag. "You'll have to help him eat all of this," she added, bumping up against his shoulder. "I made up the bed for Nicky."

"And Justin'll sleep on the couch; he doesn't care," Gary said. "Their train gets in at eleven. Should we plan to eat around three?" He looked at the food on the counter. "Or just keep it casual and let them eat when they want?"

Bernie wanted a sit-down dinner, traditional, but she knew his children weren't accustomed to that. "Whatever they want, babe. I have plenty of vegetables for Nicky. I'll just set everything out," she said.

"I'm glad I had the chance to talk to each of them already about the job; gave it a little time to sink in," Gary said. Bernie chopped thyme and sliced lemons – she'd stuffed them into the two chickens she planned to roast. Of course, now there were chicken wings; maybe Justin wouldn't want her roast chicken. Nicole would likely eat only vegetables, maybe some tofu. But at least she was eating, Bernie thought. And she had told Gary she didn't care what everyone else ate.

"So, Hugh had no trouble getting this place sublet?" She finished stuffing the chickens, laid them side by side in a roasting pan, and managed to find room in the refrigerator to keep the pan until it was time to put it in the oven.

"The new professor arrives a few days after New Year's. She's the new chair of the Medieval Studies Department, which I understand is very popular." He rolled his eyes. "Medieval Studies is popular, but no one wants to study German anymore. Figure that one out."

"There's no explaining it, love. Let it go. We have our own new adventure in front of us." She filled a large bowl with water and ice and started to peel carrots.

Gary pulled her away. "The kids' train doesn't arrive for another hour."

"Gary, the carrots!" She laughed and tossed them in the bowl as he led her out of the kitchen.

***

Karl sat on a stool in the kitchen and watched as Ella pulled a roast from the oven. She spooned juices over the crisp brown meat and his nose tingled with the smell. He inhaled deeply and wondered if he'd lose that sense, and hoped it would be the last thing to go. As she slid the pan back on the rack and closed the oven, the doorbell rang. Before either of them could call out, Paul opened the door and lumbered in, with Sophie right behind him.

"*Joyeux Noël!*" he boomed.

Ella wiped her hands on her apron and ran to her son. He towered over Ella and as his huge arms encircled her, he lifted her off the floor. Karl rose slowly and made his way to the foyer just as Paul set his mother back on her feet. His eyes took in his son's casual appearance, and he bit down on his tongue to keep from saying anything. He didn't want to ruin the day for Ella, who was so happy to have Paul and Sophie in the house. Sophie handed Ella a miniature Christmas tree, decorated with tiny silver ornaments.

"Thank you, Sophie," she murmured, taking the tree and placing it on the counter. Karl moved to inspect it, and saw that the silver ornaments were just plastic, painted to look silver. He scratched his chin and held out his hand to Paul.

"Good to see you, son. Merry Christmas."

Paul's grip felt as if it might crush the bones in his hand. Karl winced inwardly, but said nothing. Finally Paul loosened his grip and pushed stringy hair back from his wide forehead. Karl stared at his son and pictured the face of his other son, the handsome, well-groomed Jean-Michel Eicher. He turned away and sat heavily in a chair.

"Sophie, how are you feeling?" Ella had Sophie's thin arm through hers. They moved to sit together on the sofa.

"I'm fine," she said in a voice that was as whispery as rain. Karl peered at the girl. Sophie's hair was shaved on the sides of her head but long everywhere else. She'd stuck some kind of gel in it and combed it back from her forehead. One of those barbell things pierced through an eyebrow, and a ring of roses was tattooed around her neck, like a choker. Karl shuddered internally and hoped Dani would arrive soon.

"How are you, Dad?" Paul wedged his massive bulk into one of the fine upholstered chairs Ella had chosen to complement the room's décor.

Karl glanced at Ella, who made the slightest movement of her head to signal *no, don't say it yet. Dani's not here.* After all their years together, he recognized the little signs from his wife.

"Well, your grandmother's death came as quite a shock to all of us. I'm sorry there was no service, but it was what she wanted. And I chose to honor her last request." Karl's fingers grasped at the fabric on the chair's arm.

"Yeah, sorry about that. I wouldn't have been able to leave the shop anyway." Paul leaned forward and stuck his giant hand into a glass bowl filled with assorted nuts.

"Leave them alone!" Karl bellowed at his son. Paul's hand opened and the nuts fell back into the bowl. Everything froze: Paul's hand hovered above the low table, Sophie's mouth dropped open, and Ella stiffened. Karl's fingers continued to massage the fabric on the chair, and he looked to Ella. "I'm sorry. Ella, I guess this would be a good time to tell them then."

Ella stood and gripped the back of Karl's chair. "Your father didn't mean to yell, Paul," she said in a measured voice. Karl closed his eyes; he didn't want to look in his son's face.

"What is it? What's wrong?" Paul withdrew his hand from the bowl of nuts.

Before Ella could say anything, Dani burst through the front door, bringing the cold December air with her.

"*Joyeux Noël!*" she exclaimed. Karl opened his eyes and grinned. Dani teetered in on impossibly high heels, balancing brightly-wrapped packages in her arms. "Mama, take these, please, before I drop them."

"Dani, darling," Karl said, tipping his head back as she kissed both of his cheeks. "We are all here now."

Dani exchanged kisses with her mother, brother, sister-in-law, and finally turned back to her father. She searched his eyes and frowned. "Papa, what is it? What's wrong?" She laid her hand on his shoulder.

"Dani, sit, please," Ella said. Dani took the spot next to Sophie and raised her eyebrows at Paul. He shrugged in return. "Your father has something to say to all of you. Karl?"

Karl, sitting across from his family, winced. He looked at each of them in turn, searing an image into his brain. His beautiful, loving wife, forgiving, caring. His daughter-in-law, thin and pale, but devoted to Paul, and soon to be the mother of his child. Paul, his son, marching to his own beat, which Karl had to admire. And Dani, his little girl, all grown up now, a vision in dark purple. His news would break her heart.

Karl pressed the heel of his hand to his forehead. "This is difficult, and if I can't do it, your mother will step in."

"Karl..." Ella's voice faltered.

"You are my family," he said. "I want you to listen carefully. Paul. Dani. I have a disease. It's called Huntington's. It's not too bad now, but it's going to get a lot worse. Sometimes I have little control over what I say. Sometimes I forget little things. I'll die, of course, but I don't know when. Hopefully not too soon. Apparently I inherited the disease from my father, who died before exhibiting any of the symptoms. And because I inherited it, you two have a fifty percent chance of having inherited it, too." He paused and licked his lips. His throat felt thick and he swallowed a couple of times. Ella seemed to read his mind and brought a cup of water.

He continued. "You can be tested to find out if you are carrying the gene. You should find out, especially you," he pointed to Paul, "with a baby on the way. If you don't have the specific gene, you'll never get the disease, and your kids will never get it, either. Ella, more water, please."

There was silence. "Wait," said Dani. "What? Is this like cancer, Papa?"

"No!" Karl roared. "Dammit, Dani, listen to me for once! It's Huntington's. Hunt. Ing. Ton's. Okay? Look it up if you don't know what it is." He'd never spoken so sharply to his daughter. Karl stared at her before mumbling, "Again, I'm sorry."

His daughter looked away from him. "Thank you, Papa. I think I've got that."

Ella brought Karl his water and stood away from him. "As you have probably guessed, one of the symptoms of the disease is an outburst like that. It can't be helped."

"Can't be helped," Karl said quietly as he sipped.

"This disease has a slow progress," Ella continued. "The decision to have the test is up to you. No one can decide for you. They won't just administer the test; you'd have to have weeks or months of counseling first. And there's one more thing, something important." She turned to Karl. "Is it all right if I tell them?"

Karl nodded, his head bowed in defeat.

"About thirty years ago, while I was pregnant with you, Paul, your father had a very brief affair with a university student in Fribourg. It resulted in a pregnancy, and the woman had a son. Your father didn't know about the pregnancy or the birth until about five years ago, when this woman visited him unexpectedly." Karl watched her speak, and saw the muscles in her face tighten. Of course it was still painful for her, he thought.

"That's when you threw him out of the house," Paul said, reaching for more nuts, ignoring his father as if he were an inanimate object set on a chair.

Ella kept her eyes on Karl. "Yes," she said, nodding. "We separated because of it, but I've forgiven your father and we are together, no matter what. After Papa went to see the doctor, and learned about the disease, he contacted the boy's mother, Bernadette."

"How did you find her?" Dani asked, narrowing her eyes at her father. He pressed his index finger to the twitch under his eye and let Ella answer.

"We found her through Dr. Schmidt, who cared for both her and me during our pregnancies. Bernadette contacted her son and gave him your father's telephone number and address, and he came here last week."

Dani was shaking her head back and forth.

"Dani, what is it?" Ella asked.

"We have a brother," she whispered. She looked over to Paul. "We have a brother," she repeated. "And he's the same age as you."

"Yeah," he mumbled. "Where is he? Around here?" Paul directed the questions to his mother. Karl's eyes flitted from his son to his wife, while the rest of his body stayed motionless.

"He lives in Fribourg. He's married, and has children. I think he'll take the test," Ella said, with a glance to Karl. "That's what he said."

"I'd like to meet him," Dani said. "He's my brother, we should meet, get to know each other. If that's okay with you, Mama. And I definitely want to be tested. If I have this disease, I want to know." She stood and walked to the kitchen.

"Not me," said Paul, and Sophie jerked her head toward him. "I don't want to know about that." He stuck his hand into the nut bowl again, although there were few nuts left.

"Paul, think about the baby Sophie is carrying," Ella pleaded.

"Please, Paul," Sophie said. Her eyes were round as plates.

Karl wiped his eyes with shaky hands. "Can we have dinner, please? Before Paul eats all the nuts?"

***

It was a quiet Christmas dinner in the Eicher household. The male nurse Michel had hired to assist his father had arrived thirty minutes earlier. Michel directed him to the house next door and instructed him to wash and dress Bruno. Lucia asked Klara to help in the kitchen, getting her out of their house while the nurse attended to Bruno. When the nurse knocked on their door twenty minutes later, Klara ran to it and flung it open. Michel could see that his father was shaved, combed, and dressed in clean clothes. He looked good.

"Thank you," Michel murmured as the nurse escorted Bruno to the dining room table. "Please stay and eat with us. Lucia, set an extra place for Nils, would you?"

Before Nils took one bite of food, he fed Bruno, carefully and methodically. Bruno ate all of his food in silence, and conversation was minimal, interrupted only when Jean-Bernard piped up with a commentary on the ham or the Brussels sprouts. He adored the former, loathed the latter. Luca giggled in his high chair, his loving eyes trained on his older brother.

"Mama, you're quiet. Is the food all right?"

Klara looked up from her full plate, and Michel saw how much his mother had aged. All the time she'd been devoting to Bruno had left no time to care for herself, and it showed in her appearance. Gray skin bulged beneath her eyes, which were lifeless and pale. Her hair was nearly all silver and pinned up hastily. Michel had suggested that Lucia take Klara to the salon with her, let her be pampered before Christmas. No, Klara had said, it is not necessary. Life was all about Papa for Mama, Michel knew that. Still, he was afraid the stress and anxiety would overwhelm her. The sooner they moved to Geneva, the better.

"Everything is wonderful, my son." She gave him a thin smile and turned to Lucia. "It is delicious!" Michel eyed his mother's plate. Klara had barely touched her food. She glanced at Bruno, who stared at the salt shaker on the table. He didn't even know his own family anymore, and a few mini-strokes had taken away his ability to speak. The nurse spoon-fed him small portions of pureed food from the plate and murmured words of encouragement in German.

"The movers arrive on Monday, Mama. I can help you tomorrow and over the weekend with packing boxes." Klara nodded and Michel saw tears spill from her downcast eyes. "Oh, Mama."

She wiped her cheeks and waved away his words. "I'm just a silly old woman, Michel. It's been a long time living here. Since we first brought you home as a little baby. But I'll be fine. And your Papa, he won't even know the difference," she added, her voice breaking.

Michel ran his hand over his close-cropped hair. "Mama, we would stay if we could, you know that. I need this job; there isn't anything here in Fribourg." It was true; Michel had walked to the Eurotel the day he had the first meeting with Almazi and McDonald, but they weren't looking for a manager. And all the other hotels were smaller than the Hotel de la Rose. They couldn't pay anywhere near the salary he'd had, let alone the salary he'd been offered by Almazi.

"We'll all be fine in Geneva, Mama," Lucia said with an encouraging smile. "Won't we, Jean-Bernard? All together!"

"Yes, Mama, all together! *Nonna*, please don't cry," the little boy said. He pulled his small stuffed horse from under his chair and offered it to his grandmother. "You can hold Max if you want, *Nonna*." He looked up at Klara with big brown eyes, and she softened. Pulling him onto her lap, she said in a muffled voice, "Oh, my little love, as long as we're all together, I am happy." She kissed his forehead and Jean-Bernard grinned. Michel exhaled and resumed eating.

He hadn't told Klara anything about showing up at Karl Berset's house in Lausanne. He hadn't said a word about Karl having Huntington's, or the imminent genetic testing. He was right to keep these things from her. In her fragile state, he didn't think she could handle any more worry. Even if it turned out that he had the marker, an indicator that he would develop Huntington's one day, he wasn't sure he'd tell her. He glanced at his father, now finished with his meal. The blissful state of ignorance, he thought. We are all in pain, Papa, he said to himself, but you are simply drifting back to a childlike state.

The nurse stood and helped Bruno to his feet. "I take him back now and put him to bed," Nils stated. At that, Klara pushed away her plate and stood also.

"Mama, you stay here and finish eating. Nils can handle it," Michel said, putting a hand over his mother's. "Relax. I'll go over there in a few minutes. Then we'll have some of Lucia's tiramisu."

"Let me heat your plate," Lucia said, but Klara raised her hand. "It's fine. Such a wonderful meal, Lucia." She put a few forkfuls of food into her mouth and chewed silently.

The boys were finished eating and wanted to play with their new toys. Lucia escorted them into the living room and set them up.

"Mama, would you like to lie down in our room? Perhaps you need a little nap," Michel said to his mother. "Just to rest your eyes. I know it's been an emotional day."

"I wonder if it will be the last Christmas with your father," Klara said softly. She pushed back her chair. "I should help Lucia to clean up the dishes."

"Mama, please. It's hard now, I know. I wish we didn't have to move, either. I love Fribourg. Geneva's a big city. But we'll be together. You and Lucia will discover Geneva together." He hesitated, then decided to say it. "And Mama, if Papa would be better in a home..."

Klara shook her head. "How can I do that to him?" Her eyes were wet.

"If he is in a place where he receives very good care, all the time, it means that you would not be so tired, so worried about him, and you can visit every day. Most important is Papa's care, yes?"

Klara nodded. "Yes, of course. I don't want you or Lucia to have extra burden."

Lucia returned to sit at the table and glanced at Michel, who nodded.

"Papa is not a burden, and neither are you. You are my parents also." She paused. "Mama, I'm pregnant again."

Klara's hands flew to her face. "Oh! Oh, Lucia! What news on Christmas!" She grasped Lucia's hands and squeezed. "Did you just find out?"

Lucia nodded. "It's only three months. We're both very happy about it. Maybe a little girl this time?" Michel was happy to see his mother's face soften, her eyes brighten.

"Yes, maybe a little girl this time," she whispered, looking around. The boys played quietly in the living room, making truck noises.

Lucia grinned. "Let's start thinking about girl names."

Klara laid her hand against Lucia's fair cheek. "You are just like a daughter to me, you know."

"I love you, too," Lucia said.

Michel blinked hard and cleared his throat. "I'll go next door to check on Papa," he said and hurried out the door.

Chapter Eleven

From their apartment on Hutterweg, Gary and Bernie looked out across the river to the university on the opposite side. White lights framed the roof of one tall building, and twinkled in the branches of a tree nearby. A light snow had fallen the previous evening and dusted the trees that lined the banks of the river.

There was a bottle of good champagne chilling in the refrigerator, and Bernie had prepared a platter of meats, cheeses, and fruits. While most of Innsbruck reveled this New Year's Eve, Gary and Bernie intended to spend a quiet evening inside.

The apartment was compact but efficient, and anyway, Gary thought, they were used to living in small spaces. Yesterday they walked to the campus, and Bernie had grown frustrated with the unimaginably long street names.

"How will I ever remember them without you?" she'd cried. Gary had laughed and pulled her closer.

"Use landmarks instead, love. Look, after we leave the apartment, we turn left. The yellow building is on our left, okay?" She nodded. "Good. Then walk straight ahead, past the bank, and turn left down the next street. That leads directly to the footbridge."

"Yes, right," Bernie had said, her breath making steamy little puffs in front of her mouth.

"Now, we've crossed the bridge and here we are on the Innrain. That's the main street and leads to the university. Here, we'll stop at Tyrolis for coffee and you'll remember."

"I'm just being dumb," Bernie had muttered, shaking her head. "I shouldn't be so intimidated by German."

"It's all still new," Gary replied, pulling her close for a kiss before they entered the coffee shop.

Now, as the minutes fell away and the new year approached, Gary basked in this new chapter of their lives. They were creating it together, and 2009 promised to be a very special year.

"Would you like to go to Fribourg this weekend?" Bernie asked. "Before we left New York, I sent emails to both Hanna and Michael to let them know we were moving here. I didn't hear back from Michael, but Hanna wrote. Gary, she was so happy! She invited us to her house for the weekend." She wondered if Michael had contacted Karl Berset, and if perhaps that was the reason she couldn't reach him.

"Babe, I'd love to, but I can't. Not with all the preparation I have to do before classes start up. Actually, day after tomorrow I have a meeting with the Vice Dean, with Human Resources, lots of paperwork. Sorry, honey. But you should go. I won't be around much, anyway." He poured champagne and handed a tall flute to his wife. She took the glass and stared out the window for a long time.

"Where are your thoughts, Bernadette?" Gary stood behind her, his glass in hand, ready to toast the new year. She turned to him.

"I'm right here with you, love," she said. She glanced at her watch. Almost midnight.

They opened the sliding door and stepped out onto a small balcony to watch the fireworks display over the old town. It was freezing outside, and Gary wrapped a big blanket around their shoulders.

"We'll be so happy here, I just know it," he whispered to her. "This is a new beginning, the start of a memorable year."

"Beautiful," she said, her breath making smoky curlicues in the frigid air. Gary pulled her closer so she could draw his body heat into her.

They watched the fireworks explode in the dark sky, creating streamers of light and color followed by puffs of smoke. She could hear the cheering in the Hofgarten, at the edge of the old town. Earlier that afternoon, she and Gary had walked there, taking the route along the river.

The fireworks ended, the cheering subsided, and Gary and Bernie returned to the warmth of their apartment. "Happy New Year, my Bernie," Gary murmured into her neck. "I love you more than words can express."

"Happy New Year, my Gary," she echoed. "I couldn't be happier than I am at this very moment."

***

Karl and Ella had a serious talk. Although he said he wasn't ready to give up working, Ella persuaded him to notify the bank's management that he would work through the end of January and then retire.

"Karl, don't you want to maintain your dignity? Walk out of there with your head held high? I don't want it to get to the point that you're unable to function properly. Everyone in that office respects you, and I don't want this disease to change any of that in their minds."

Reluctantly, he'd agreed with her, even if he knew that not everyone in the office respected him. After discovering that his mother had died nearly penniless, he thought he would work for another five years, until he was sixty-five years old. It was true; he'd been counting on an inheritance. Perhaps that was foolish, but he had no idea where all the money had gone. There were no gambling casinos in Lausanne, although he learned there was one in Geneva. It was possible she'd frequented the casino in Meyrin. Or perhaps she had made bad investment decisions. Karl realized he would have known about the losses if he had spent more time with his mother, if he had been more invested in what she was doing. But she valued her independence.

And he was busy working, and mending his relationship with Ella. Now it was too late. Mathilde Berset's fortune was all gone.

"Dani said she's going to have the test. I wish Paul would reconsider." He held her hand under the blanket.

"Paul does what he wants, Karl, he always has. He didn't listen to you when you suggested university, or a job in your bank. He has his own mind."

"I understand, but he also has Sophie, and a baby to come. He should think about his family more than himself." *I'm such a hypocrite,* Karl thought.

"You can't force it, *cheri*. Dani will be tested, and it seemed as though Jean-Michel wants to know, too."

"Yes. He is a fine boy, Jean-Michel, didn't you think so, Ella? Of course I want that everyone will have a negative result." He sighed heavily. "But the odds are that at least one of the three will carry the gene. I wish this disease on no one."

"Don't think about that now. It's a new year. 2009. May we have many blessings." She leaned over to kiss her husband. "Try to sleep now. Happy New Year, my love."

"Happy New Year, my Ella." He turned away from her and pulled the blanket up to his neck. Within minutes, he could hear his wife's light rhythmic snoring. His thoughts, tangled and jumpy, kept sleep at bay for hours.

***

Michel and his family were finally settled in the new house. True to his promise, Gamil Almazi had found them a very nice residence in Cologny, on Lake Geneva. The villa was owned by Almazi Holdings and Michel would rent it directly from the company, for a very reasonable price, commensurate with his salary. Michel didn't know a lot about real estate, but he guessed that the villa, with six bedrooms and four bathrooms, would normally rent for three or four times what he'd been asked to pay. He didn't like being dependent on Almazi, but there wasn't time to argue. He would rent the villa for at least six months, but he and Lucia agreed to start looking around next month for a place of their own.

Gamil also procured a male nurse for Bruno; in fact, Klara and Bruno had a separate wing in the villa, assuring privacy for all. The male nurse, Ahmed, lived in a guest house on the property and attended to Bruno during the day. Klara was relieved she didn't have to place him in a nursing home, and every day she asked Michel to express her gratitude to "Monsieur Almazi."

It was New Year's Eve, and Michel didn't have to report for work until Monday. He was glad to have the weekend to acclimate himself and his family to their new house and neighborhood. He didn't own a car, and the bus ride into the city was nearly forty minutes. Gamil told Michel that a car would pick him up each morning and bring him to the hotel.

"Do you think we need to buy a car, Michel?" Lucia asked that morning, over a breakfast of fluffy croissants and hot coffee. She tore off a piece of croissant, smeared strawberry jam inside, and popped it in her mouth.

"I hope not," he said. "I don't know how to drive; neither do you. Listen, Lulu, I think we stay here for a few months, until the springtime, but we look for a place of our own. Someplace perhaps closer to the city and the hotel. We don't need such a big house. I'm grateful to Gamil for this place, of course, and the rent is very low, so in six months' time we should have some money saved, for our own house. The rent from the house in Fribourg will help." Actually, it hadn't been difficult to find renters for the house. A young couple wanted to live on one side, and the woman's parents would occupy the other. A situation very similar to Michel and Lucia's.

"Let's ask Mama if she wants to go to the city with us. We'll take the boys. Ahmed is with Papa." Bruno seemed comfortable with Ahmed. Probably someone's nephew, Michel thought, although Gamil had provided his credentials, and Ahmed spoke fluent English and French, and passable German. As long as Bruno was calm and seemed at ease, Michel was satisfied. Perhaps a trip into the city would do everyone good. The house was massive, overwhelming, and Michel knew Klara would enjoy spoiling the boys with sweets at a *confiserie*.

"Sure, we'll take the bus." Michel thought

about his upcoming appointment with the genetic counseling agency. It was at the end of next week, a Friday evening after work. He hoped to see Karl again, perhaps meet his children and find out what they were planning to do. But that would have to wait; he was preparing for his first full week at the new job, and tending to his own family. "But we won't stay long, Lulu. I want us all to be back in the house before it gets dark."

"Michel, stop worrying! It's New Year's Eve."

"There are people who pull pranks tonight, you know. It's not all about the fireworks. We can watch the light show from the comfort of home. Geneva is not the same as Fribourg. So come on then, call the boys." He pulled on his coat and picked up the telephone to call his mother, because it would take five minutes just to walk to the other end of the house.

They boarded a bus near their home, and forty minutes later they all arrived in downtown Geneva.

"The parties in Old Town don't start until well after ten o'clock," Michel murmured, looking at a colorful flyer tacked onto a public bulletin board across from the bus station. "That won't work," he added. Thinking quickly, he took Jean-Bernard's little hand and said, "Come on, *p'tit*, we'll see what they're planning for later." Michel led the way, as Lucia and Klara pushed Luca in a stroller.

Halfway up the street, Michel stopped when he heard a vaguely familiar voice call his name.

"Jean-Michel!" He turned to see Farid Almazi, Gamil's brother. Farid leaned against the façade of the Palais Marcotte, an upscale hotel and restaurant. A woman stood next to him smoking a cigarette. She looked like a supermodel, in a full-length fur coat and high-heeled boots. Long blond hair streamed out from under a fur hat, and oversized black sunglasses covered much of her face, even though the day was overcast.

Michel turned to Lucia and whispered, "That's Gamil's brother. I'll be right back." He left his family standing on the sidewalk as he hurried over to say hello to Farid. Michel had no intention of dragging his wife, children, and mother over to meet Farid and his companion, who Michel assumed was another high-end call girl. As he extended his hand in greeting, it dawned on him that Farid was a pimp. But before he could react to this realization, Farid gripped his hand and shook it hard.

"Jean-Michel, how are you? Happy New Year! 2009 almost here now." Farid ignored the woman standing next to him, who turned away and blew smoke into the air. Michel watched as she threw the cigarette to the pavement and crushed it under the pointy toe of her boot.

"Thank you, Farid, and the same to you." Michel glanced back at Lucia, who was speaking with Klara. "Anyway, I'm with my family, so I should go."

"Very nice. You have two boys. That is very good. You know, Dani asked about you. She would very much like to see you again. I'll make arrangements." His eyes darkened as his lips curled upwards in a teasing smirk.

"Oh, I don't know," Michel stammered. "She was very nice, but..." He glanced back again at his wife, who was now giving him a stern look.

"Yes, she said you two got along very well," Farid said with a laugh. "Gamil wants a happy and satisfied employee. Dani satisfied you, yes?"

Michel opened his mouth to explain, but paused. He didn't want to get Dani in trouble. Farid had no doubt covered her "fees" that evening, and if he found out that nothing had transpired, it could be bad for Dani. Michel trusted his gut instinct and said nothing about the pretty dark-haired girl. "Farid, I really must go. Happy New Year." He turned away.

"Happy New Year! I will be in touch," Farid called.

Michel didn't turn back.

"Come, Lulu, we take the boys for a sweet, and then we will return to the house." He pulled his wife's hand sharply.

"Michel, stop." Lucia stood firm and glared at her husband. "That was rude. You didn't even introduce us. That was your boss's brother?" She stamped her foot, although Michel wasn't sure if it from the cold or from her anger.

"Lulu, he was drunk." It was a lie, but Michel was sure Lucia couldn't tell one way or the other. "I didn't want to embarrass you or Mama. I don't work for him. I work for Gamil. Farid is useless. Please, let's take the boys to the old town." He started walking, and she allowed herself to be pulled along.

"Everything is alright?" Klara asked, pushing the stroller alongside them while Lucia held Jean-Bernard's hand.

"Fine, Mama. Everything is fine." Michel stared straight ahead.

Chapter Twelve

"You sure you'll be okay without me?" Bernie finished packing a weekend's worth of items into a small bag. "I'll be back late on Sunday."

Gary kissed her on the nose. "Of course, sweetie. I'll spend the weekend preparing for classes, and you won't be here to distract me."

Bernie rolled her eyes and tickled his beard. "I'm looking forward to seeing Hanna. She'll be sorry to miss you. She really likes you, you know."

"And what about Michael?" Gary opened his briefcase and retrieved a pile of papers. He laid them on the small kitchen table, which also served as his workspace.

Bernie shook her head, auburn curls bouncing everywhere. "I didn't hear back from him. Thinking perhaps he and Lucia spent the holidays in Italy with her family."

"So the last time you spoke with him was weeks ago, right?"

"Yeah, when I called him about Karl. I have no idea how he's processing this information.

Whether he met with Karl, what was said." She chewed on her lip before speaking again. "It's a worry, Gary. He could be carrying the gene, which would mean he'd get the disease. And potentially pass it on to his children. But I also know it's a matter for Michael and Lucia, and his parents if he chooses to tell them."

"Still." He cupped her shoulders and pulled her closer. "Listen, once you speak with him, you'll feel better. I know you're not one to let an uncertainty rule your world. You'll talk to him, and find out." His voice was muffled against her soft neck. "Come on, we'll go to the station together."

"No, Gary, I can walk there. You have too much to do."

"Not so much that I can't walk my wife to the train station," he said, taking a step back. "I'm the one who's carrying your luggage." He zipped the bag and picked it up.

They strolled past shops still decorated with Christmas displays. Gary breathed in deeply. "We might have snow today," he said, casting a glance upwards to a steely sky.

They arrived at the station and Gary walked Bernie to the concrete platform. The train would arrive from the east, having originated in Vienna.

"Give my love to Hanna," he said, "and let me know if you speak with Michael. What time do you arrive in Fribourg?"

"Three this afternoon," Bernie said. "I'll call you to let you know when I arrive back on Sunday. You have a good weekend, darling." She smiled, but Gary could tell she was concerned. He touched her cheek one last time and she boarded the train. As the doors closed, he waved until he knew she couldn't see him anymore.

Gary thought about his own children, and understood Bernie's worry. If Michael carried the gene for Huntington's, it would be devastating, for him, for his family, and for Bernadette. He hoped she'd be able to make contact with her son in Fribourg.

***

Once Karl had made the difficult decision to tender his resignation, on the first Monday of the new year, he planned a day off on Friday so he could meet with his lawyer. Since there was no money from his mother, he'd have to ensure that Ella would be financially secure once he was gone. He had no idea how much longer he'd live, but he expected to be incapacitated within a year or two. His doctor had told him that Huntington's could progress at varying speeds; sometimes the disease wasn't full blown for ten years, but the way Karl felt lately, he assumed it would be sooner than that. Dani was doing well; her modeling career had really taken off and she seemed to have plenty of money. Paul, on the other hand, would likely always be struggling. It was his choice of careers, Karl thought bitterly. He should work harder, with Sophie and a baby on the way, maybe finish school. Do something more than run a tattoo shop. After all, Karl thought, it was just a fad. And how many tattoos could one person have? Paul said he had sixteen tattoos, or "tats," as he referred to them. The entire length of both arms, one on each calf, something on his neck, his shoulders, above his left breast, and God knows where else. Karl didn't want to know. If Sophie had any, they were hidden. And he'd never even asked Dani. He prayed she hadn't marred her beautiful body with ink.

Dani should have a boyfriend, he thought. Someone successful, wealthy, to take care of her. If she did have the Huntington's marker, she'd need someone, but she should settle down soon. Karl tried to consider who he knew; perhaps one of his friends had a son? Dani was planning to meet with the genetic counselor in the middle of the month. And if she did have the marker, then she'd never want to find a husband. There wasn't enough time. But perhaps he could get someone interested in her. Who? He thought about it as he waited in the lawyer's office. *Wait!* He snapped his fingers, and the receptionist gave a start.

"I hope that wasn't directed at me," she said sharply. Karl shook his head and gave her his most winning smile. "I just remembered something," he said by way of explanation. But his magic didn't work on this one, he realized. She twisted her mouth with disdain and lowered her head. *She has no idea how wonderful it is to remember*, he thought.

Raphael has a brother, he repeated to himself. His lawyer was a longtime friend of the family, and had even provided some mediation assistance when Karl raised the topic of divorce. Not that Raphael had fixed their marriage, but he'd invited them both to the office to talk. And it did begin the healing process.

Karl recalled Raphael talking about a younger brother, unmarried. A dentist? He couldn't remember, but he would definitely ask if he ever managed to get into the office.

"Monsieur Berset," the receptionist said in flat, dull voice, as if she wanted to be anywhere else but there, in that chair, at that desk, calling out his name. Karl rose from the chair and glared at her as he passed. "Thank you so much," he said with exaggerated sincerity. He walked down the short corridor to Raphael's office.

"Karl!" Raphael Klug spread his fat arms. His girth had expanded since the last time Karl had seen him, and his round, pink face reminded Karl of a baby's bottom. "So good to see you! Please, have a seat."

Raphael Klug was a top lawyer, but on first impression, he looked like a buffoon, with his clownish ways. Karl saw his shirt buttons strained against his stomach and wondered if they might just pop off. Karl opened his mouth to suggest a diet, but stopped himself before he spoke. He knew that inappropriateness was one of the symptoms of Huntington's, and there would come a time, Karl imagined, when he'd just say whatever was on his mind, regardless of whether the time was right. For now, he stayed silent.

"Thanks for making time for me, Rafe."

"I'm sorry about your mother, Karl." Rafe pursed his rubbery lips and slid a fat finger under his shirt collar. "What happened to all her money?"

"I don't know," he said, with a small kick. He saw Rafe's eyes follow the foot. "It's a symptom. Twitching, kicking. Sometimes I say things I shouldn't." He watched as Rafe's cheeks flushed a deeper pink. "Listen, I need you to look at everything I have. Ella wants me to retire at the end of the month. If I'm going to do that, I'll need to tell them on Monday."

Rafe spread his chubby hands. Hands that were as soft like a little girl's, squishy and moist. "I'm heading to Geneva this weekend with my brother." He winked at Karl. "A little getaway for the boys. You should come with us!"

Karl's shoulders sagged with an invisible weight. "No thanks. Those days are done for me." He looked up. "How is your brother, anyway? Still single?"

Rafe nodded. "But he's looking to settle down. Just can't meet the right girl."

"He's not seeing anyone right now?"

"No one special," Rafe said. "Why? You have a girl for him?"

"What about Dani?"

"Little Dani?" Rafe laughed, a high-pitched, girly giggle. "She's just a baby, Karl." He stopped laughing when he saw Karl's face.

"You haven't seen her lately, my friend. She's all grown up, and a knockout. And I want to see her married."

Rafe shuffled his feet. Karl looked down at the man's improbably small feet, clad in shiny black shoes. "Look, Darek is thirty years old..."

"Dani is twenty," Karl interrupted. "At least let's have them meet. Okay? After that, it's up to them. We stay out of it."

Raphael peered at Karl, who stared back. "Okay, Karl, okay. When we return next week. And hold off on the job until I can get a full report to you. By Wednesday, Thursday, okay?"

Karl stood, unsteady for just a moment. "Sure. Okay, Rafe, thanks. Have fun in Geneva." He turned to the door, and paused. "Dani is a model in Geneva, you know. High fashion."

He saw Rafe's squinty little pig eyes widen and smiled as he walked out of the office, knowing Rafe would be on the phone to Darek in a matter of seconds.

***

"I'm so glad you don't start work until Monday," Lucia said. She placed a plate in front of Michel: scrambled eggs, a fat sausage, buttered toast. A small glass of orange juice and hot, strong coffee in a ceramic cup.

"Yes, as am I, but Gamil has called me in today anyway." He saw the disappointment in his wife's eyes. "Not until mid-afternoon, but Lulu, there's a lot to learn about this hotel, and if I want to have a weekend at home, I must go in today." He dug in to the breakfast and murmured satisfied sounds as he ate.

"You'll be home tonight though?"

"Of course," he mumbled through a mouthful of eggs.

The doorbell rang and Lucia left the table to answer it. She returned with an envelope. "It's for you," she said. "Brought by messenger." She handed him a cream-colored envelope of heavy paper, with his name written is careful, curling script.

Michel set down his juice to slide a finger under the flap. He pulled out a folded sheet of fine stationery that felt like linen. On it was a note, written in the same deliberate script: *"My friend Daniel would like to meet you. He is only in town tonight. It is good for business. Will send car at nine. -Farid"*

Michel took a sharp intake of breath. Daniel? Dani, of course. Good for business. Did that mean Gamil endorsed it? Michel felt his breakfast rumble in his stomach. He'd like to speak with Gamil about this. Farid was way out of line, and while the girl Dani was very nice, he needed to make sure Farid understood that he wasn't interested.

"What is it?" Lucia's voice broke into his thoughts. He looked at her trusting, angelic face. She held the coffeepot out and filled his cup.

"Oh, it's an invitation of some sort. Gamil's brother, Farid? The one I spoke with on New Year's Eve? He has a friend, Daniel, apparently, who wants to meet me. Tonight." Michel's voice trailed off.

"Tonight? Oh, Michel. But you'll be in the city all afternoon."

Michel sank lower in his chair, his appetite gone, and the hot coffee burning its way down his throat. Oh, he did not like lying to Lucia. All of this was wrong. I should speak with Gamil, he thought.

"Yes, well, I'll speak with Gamil to see if it's absolutely necessary."

Lucia sighed as she sat next to him. She took his hand in hers. "*Amore*, I know this is all new. And yes, you are making more money with this new job. The house is lovely, though too big, and we are grateful for the nurse provided to care for Papa. But these people, Michel. This Farid, he is rude. He called you over to speak in Geneva and ignored us, standing on the sidewalk. He asks you to give up time with your family. And you don't work for Farid! You work for his brother."

Michel moved the remainder of his breakfast around on his plate. He wasn't even hungry anymore. "You're right, Gamil is my boss, and I will talk to him." He leaned over to kiss Lucia. "Thanks for breakfast." He stood and walked away from his wife, down a long corridor to a room he used as his office.

Michel closed the door and slumped at his desk. This had to stop, he thought. It has to stop now. He picked up the phone and replaced the receiver. Instead, he pulled his cell phone from his pocket and dialed the number for Gamil's office.

"Monsieur Almazi's office, good morning."

"Good morning. This is Jean-Michel Eicher calling for Monsieur Almazi, please."

"One moment." The line was silent as Michel waited. He wished he had some mineral water for his churning stomach.

"I'm sorry, Monsieur Eicher, Monsieur Almazi is in a meeting until ten. May I take a message?"

Michel set his jaw. "Yes, please ask him to call my cell phone as soon as possible. Thank you." He clicked off and pounded his desk. He checked the clock on the wall. Eight-thirty. He left his office, walked down another long corridor to the master suite, and laced up his running shoes. When he returned to the kitchen, Lucia was at the sink, washing up the dishes from breakfast. The boys played together on the floor with their new toys from Christmas.

"Did you speak with him?" Lucia half-turned from the soapy water in the sink.

"No, he was in a meeting," Michel muttered. "But I have my phone with me. Just going to take a walk." He was stopped by the look on her face.

"Perhaps I get the boys dressed and we can go together?"

He took two steps toward her. "Not right now, Lulu. I need to walk. Or run. I'll be back." And he headed outside before she could say anything. Before he could acknowledge the hurt look on her face.

Michel walked. Then he ran. He ran along the quay, past the park on his left and the Jet d'Eau on his right, its fountain of water reaching up to touch a blue, cloudless sky. The winter sun warmed his face and he gained speed, until he found himself standing, breathless, at the edge of the lake. He desperately wanted to keep running, until he reached the hotel, where he would run up the stairs to find Gamil. But he didn't. Michel knew protocol, and he did not know Gamil well enough to be so bold. With Monsieur Rosolen, he could always speak his mind, even when their opinions differed. With Gamil, he didn't have that confidence. At least not yet. And he didn't want to be seen lurking around his place of employment, sweaty, huffing, before he'd even begun his first official day. He turned around and began walking back, knowing he'd return in six hours, dressed like the manager he was.

Chapter Thirteen

Bernie awoke to a weak sun in a gray sky, in the bedroom where she'd lived as a student, a very pregnant student, for a few months in 1979. She turned to look through the window on her right. Bare trees couldn't camouflage the playground, but the area was silent, as it was Sunday and the last day of Christmas break. She remembered how she couldn't stand to listen to the sounds of happy children playing outside, just before she gave birth to Michael and certainly not after she'd given him up for adoption.

But she'd had a lovely time visiting with her old friend Hanna. And Hanna had filled her in on Michael's new job in Geneva, and the family's move. While she was happy for Michael, she still worried that she hadn't heard from him. So much going on in his life, she mused, twirling her hair around her finger. A new job, a new house, a new baby on the way. And now the worry that a horrific disease could be lying dormant in his body. Bernie knew it wasn't Karl's fault, but still. With an effort, she threw back the blankets and pulled on comfortable clothes for breakfast.

"It's just that now he has this news about Karl, and the new job, and Lucia pregnant again. Oh, Hanna! It's too much for me to handle, how can Michael do it?"

"He's strong, Bernie. He'll be okay. Lucia told me he wanted to have the test. Of course, there is counseling that precedes it."

"How much do you know about the procedure?"

Hanna stirred her coffee. The lines around her eyes were deeper, and her short dark hair had silver threads that glinted in the morning light. "It's not done immediately. He'll have to meet with a genetic counselor for many weeks, perhaps months. A lot of people think they want to know, but the counselor will ensure that he's making an informed decision. He probably won't have the test until late February or early March."

"I wonder if Karl's children will have it," Bernie said. "He has two, a son and a daughter. Plus Michael. Out of three children, one will surely have the marker." She took a deep breath in through her nose, and exhaled slowly through her mouth. "I can't even imagine a situation where he has the disease, Hanna."

Hanna smiled sadly. "Your love for him wouldn't change, Bernie. And Lucia is remarkably strong, you've seen her. They would deal with it. Don't obsess about something that hasn't happened yet."

Bernie laughed. "That's what Gary always says. I'm sorry he couldn't come with me, but he begins teaching tomorrow. He wanted you to know that he'd have loved to visit."

"He's happy then, to be in Innsbruck?"

"Oh, sure. I'm probably happier about that than he is! But what could he do? Losing his job at the university devastated him. It's just that no one signs up for German classes anymore, Hanna. The college was losing money; they had no choice. Or that's what they told him, anyway." She rolled her eyes. "He's grateful to have this job. And we're adjusting. A year in Innsbruck, and I'm not complaining! Perhaps we'll stay; who knows?"

"And your sister? And her family? Everyone is well?"

Bernie nodded. "They're all fine, yes. Joanie's daughters are in college, and Lou is healthy. My aunt Joan is doing great." She rapped her knuckles on the table. "Knock on wood, yes, everyone is fine."

"So, stop worrying, Bernadette!" Hanna stood and brought the cups and plates to the kitchen. "What time is your train?"

Bernie looked at her watch. "Three. I'll arrive in Innsbruck at eight tonight." She stood. "Thank you for such a wonderful weekend." She embraced her friend.

"Well, I think we take a little walk around Fribourg then, yes?"

"Yes, of course, Hanna. I can stow my bag at the station."

"We'll take the bus there first." Hanna turned and opened a cupboard. She pulled out two bars of chocolate, sleeved in bright red paper. "Still your favorite?" She winked at Bernie.

"You remembered! Yes, Giandor, still my favorite. Thank you!"

"Anytime, Bernadette. I hope you will return to visit, next time with your Gary. I'm just an old woman living alone now, and happy for the company."

"Ha! You're as beautiful as ever," Bernie said, although she had to admit, age was catching up to Hanna Schmidt. Probably around sixty now, she thought. "And you still enjoy working?"

Hanna shrugged. "Some days more than others. We'll see how this year goes. So many young girls want to keep their babies, even without a husband or a partner. And they're so young!" She patted Bernie's arm. "You did the right thing, Bernadette, you know that."

"Thirty years ago? Yes. I couldn't have raised Michael then. And Klara and Bruno did a marvelous job." She paused. "I'm sorry about Bruno. That was difficult news to hear."

"Yes. It takes a toll on poor Klara, but Lucia told me they have a private nurse, a male nurse, who attends to Bruno, so Klara has a little help."

"Good. Okay, dear Hanna, I will wash up and pack my little bag. I can be ready in thirty minutes."

"Very good, Bernadette."

After a walk down the rue de Lausanne, and a lunch at the Café du Gothard, it was time to leave.

"Hanna, I'll keep in touch. I left all my contact information on your table."

The two women kissed goodbye, and Bernie headed into the train station. As she walked up the ramp to the train platform, she pulled out her phone and composed a brief text for Gary: *Train dp @ 3. Home by 8. Love.*

***

Karl spent most of the day Sunday surfing the internet, trying to learn as much as he could about Huntington's. Perhaps if he had more information to impart to Paul, he could convince him to have the test. Perhaps. He also composed his letter of resignation from the Banque Cantonale Vaudoise. His lawyer had asked him to wait, and he would, but not past Thursday. He'd email the resignation letter to Rafe for proofreading and tender his notice on Friday the ninth. He'd end his career on the last Friday in January.

Ella was out visiting friends for the afternoon, so Karl had the house to himself.

He wanted to write his obituary – something that Ella would not be burdened with when he was gone. But when he sat in front of his computer and began typing, he didn't write his death notice. Instead, a dam inside his brain gave way and memories rushed in, and his fingers tried to keep up as he was irresistibly impelled by conscience.

Shortly before my thirtieth birthday, and just

days after my beautiful wife Ella gave me the happy news of her pregnancy, I began a flirtation with one of the young American college students. Each year there was a new flock of lovelies, and each year, for the previous four years, I'd cast my eye upon one of the pretty young things. First there was Bethany, in 1975.

Karl paused, surprised that he remembered her name. He couldn't recollect her last name, but he did call to mind the first names of each of the girls. He continued.

She looked just like I imagined all American girls to look: blonde curls and blue eyes. Dimples in her cheeks. A round, nubile body and enthusiasm for unbridled sexual activity. I had only been working at the bank for months when the American students arrived. The first time Bethany stood in front of my teller window and batted her eyelashes at me, I was consumed with a desire for her. At the time, Ella and I were engaged to be married, with a wedding planned for the following June. I took Bethany out for dinner, and found her more than willing to further our friendship.

Again he paused. How much detail should he include? Who would read this? Jean-Michel? Paul and Dani? Or perhaps no one. Karl decided to continue – even if he was writing only for himself. He smiled at the memory of Bethany, genuine and spontaneous. She was comfortable in her nakedness and Karl was sure she'd had more than a few boyfriends, by her prowess.

Bethany and I saw each other for a few

months, until just before Christmas, when I broke it off. She cried, certainly, and asked me to reconsider, but I couldn't continue the deception with Ella, who was saving herself for our wedding night. Ella never knew about Bethany, and I vowed that it would never happen again. Of course, it did. The following September brought a new group of students, and Patricia was the one who stood out. She was well-bred, I could tell, by the way she carried herself, and by the amount her father deposited each month to her bank account. Patricia had more money than any of the other students. Unlike the girls who wore blue jeans every day, Patricia was well-dressed. When I asked her if she would accompany me to dinner, she surprised me by agreeing. Our first evening ended with a kiss: a long, drawn-out kiss. I perceived that she would have gladly joined me in my bed, but she adhered to an unwritten rule that precluded her from having sex on the first date. The following week, she cooked for me in her little apartment. She had only a small hot plate and one pot, but Patricia made a meal of spaghetti, olive oil, fresh tomatoes and oregano that I still can taste. I fed her pieces of silky chocolate afterwards and our evening turned into a long night of lovemaking. Patricia was not as unbridled as Bethany, and I found her to be reserved in bed. After one night with Patricia, I was already looking at other girls.

Karl leaned back in his chair and read what he had written. Perhaps he was being unfair to Patricia, but she would never read this, so what did it matter? He recalled that one night with her, and her insistence that he shower before joining her in bed. And as soon as the lovemaking had ended, she jumped out of bed and washed him away from her pure white skin. It made him want to ravage her again and again, but she had turned away from him in bed and said she needed to sleep. He took a deep breath and resumed typing.

Mary Lou arrived in Fribourg with the 1977 group of students. By then, Ella and I had been married for over a year and were trying to conceive. It was a frustrating time, as there were days I would arrive home to our little apartment, tired and cranky, and Ella would insist we make love, because the timing was right. Mary Lou walked up to my window one day in the bank. It was around the middle of November, and she told me how lonely it was to be away from her boyfriend in America. She said she longed for male company, then she winked at me. She wasn't the prettiest girl, but there was something about her that I found most attractive. We agreed to meet for a drink that evening, and ended up making love in her narrow bed while her old deaf landlady slept in the room next door. Mary Lou was daring. She wanted me to make love to her on the train, at the university, once even standing up in the bathroom at Placette. She was insatiable, and I enjoyed the novelty of trying new positions, new places. She tended to talk a lot about her boyfriend when we were together. I never mentioned Ella, of course, and I disliked her talking about 'David' all the time. As much as the sex with Mary Lou was satisfying, I ended our relationship in January. I learned later that her David flew over in March to spend spring break with her, so it was just as well.

That led him to Bernadette. Karl knew she would prove the most difficult, and wasn't sure he was up to it that afternoon. He saved the document and set a password to protect it, to keep it from Ella's eyes should she ever use the computer.

He opened the refrigerator door and pulled out a bottle of white wine. He wondered when Ella would be home. Maybe I'm on my own tonight, he thought. He poured a glass of wine and found cheese and salami for a snack. He arranged a plate of meat and cheese, with wheat crackers. Carefully, so as not to drop anything, he placed them on the counter and took a seat on one of the stools. As the winter sun dipped low behind his house, Karl Berset ate his supper alone.

***

Michel sat quietly in his home office with the door closed. He'd made an excuse to Lucia that he needed to review some files pertaining to the job he would start tomorrow. She'd taken the boys to the guest wing to visit Klara and Bruno. Michel would be happy if they stayed there and ate. It was too hard to look at his family today.

He'd been unable to reach Gamil all day

Friday, in spite of calling again and speaking to his secretary. The "very important" afternoon meeting was conducted by one of his associates, and it was a waste of time, in Michel's opinion. A walk-through of the hotel and introductions to the staff. When his brief orientation was finished, he'd made his way to Gamil's office and approached his secretary.

"I'm so sorry, Monsieur Eicher. I did relay your message to Monsieur Almazi, but he was detained in Milano. He does have your cell number, yes?"

"Yes," Michel had answered wearily. He wouldn't hear back from Gamil, he was sure of it. Which meant he'd have to go out with Farid, like it or not. He didn't think he could risk saying no to his boss's brother. And if he saw Dani again, fine. She'd be paid again for services not rendered.

He'd had an argument with Lucia that evening, too. She wasn't happy that he was expected to go out on a Friday evening, with a man she deemed rude and crass. He never argued with his wife, ever, and this time it was bad. They'd both raised their voices, and the boys came running into the kitchen, their little faces drawn with fear. Lucia had burst into tears and taken both boys away, to the wing where his parents lived. Michel finished his supper alone and changed his clothes. When the car arrived to pick him up, she was still with his parents at the other end of the massive house, so he let himself out.

And he drank much more than he should have. What the hell, he'd thought at the time, she needs to understand that this job carries a lot more responsibilities than the old job in Fribourg. This was the big time. All the while he knew he was only making excuses for himself. But it didn't stop him from accepting drink after drink.

And then there was Dani. She appeared before him as if by magic, her shiny hair piled high on her head, her large dark eyes shimmering in the candlelight. She wore a blood-red dress with no back, and Michel tried hard not to stare. As much as he attempted to picture Lucia, with her soft belly and easy smile, Dani, angular and edgy, gave him a nervous thrill. The more he hated himself for it, the more he drank.

"Will you come with me?" she had asked, offering her hand. Out of the corner of his eye, Michel saw Farid nodding at her. With an icy look at Farid, Michel wrapped his arm around Dani's bare back and whispered to her, "Take me away from this."

She'd brought him back to the same room, her room, he surmised. Where she brought her customers.

"How many?" he asked, stumbling to the leather sofa in the middle of the large room. He sank into it and Dani knelt before him, loosening his tie and helping him out of his jacket. She was blurry and soft in front of him. He tried to imagine she was his Lucia, but they were just so different. Dani was as thin as rain. He traced a finger down her raised backbone and felt her shudder.

"How many what?" she asked, playing with buttons on his shirt.

"How many men have you brought up here?" He leaned back and stared at her.

"What does it matter?" She giggled, and opened the first three buttons. Her fingers danced across his chest, until he took hold of her hand and pushed it away.

"I'm drunk, Dani. So drunk that I would easily make a mistake with you. I'm married. And I love my wife. And my kids. So, while you're beautiful and tempting and willing and, God, beautiful, I can't." He sighed loudly. "I would hate myself even more than I do right now."

Dani moved to a corner of the sofa and tucked her feet underneath her. "Okay, Jean-Michel, if that's what you want. But you know, Farid thinks we are…doing things. Why don't you just tell him that you're not interested?"

Michel looked around for water. Anything but liquor, he thought. Seeming to read his mind, Dani pulled a bottle from the refrigerator and handed it to him. He took a long drink before speaking.

"I've tried to tell his brother, my new boss. In fact, I begin my new job on Monday. I didn't know if this was part of the deal. And I've picked up that Farid doesn't like to hear the word 'no.'" Michel clasped his head with both hands. "I'm so tired, Dani. I have a lot on my mind."

She moved to sit on the wide arm of his

chair, and wrapped a thin arm across his broad shoulders. "Do you want to talk about it? I can listen, too, you know."

He turned to her. Her face, so close, her perfume, so heady, her lips, so full and... He pulled away from her and moved to the spot she'd just vacated on the sofa. He lifted his feet and stretched out. *So tired*, he thought. He closed his eyes.

He had awoken with a start, unable to remember where he was. He was alone, on a leather sofa. And then he remembered. He sat up quickly, checked to see that his clothes were all intact. Where was she?

"Dani?" he called. No answer. He looked at his watch. *Shit.* Two in the morning. He pulled his phone from his pocket. Two missed calls from Lucia. And a text message. *"Worried. Pls call."*

He had to get home. He pulled on his jacket, buttoned his shirt, stuffed his tie into a pocket, and practically ran out of the building. There were taxis, thank goodness, because it was a Friday night in Geneva. For the first time since he'd left Fribourg, he was grateful to be in the city. He hailed a cab and gave the driver his address in Cologny.

The house was dark and quiet. Michel stopped in the kitchen and pulled a bottle of Coke from the refrigerator. Gulping down the liquid, he tried to think of what he would tell Lucia in the morning. What reason could he give for being out until two in the morning? And not telephoning her? God, he hated the lies. It wasn't fair to her. It wasn't good for them. Could he tell her he'd misplaced his phone? Didn't receive the calls? Had too much to drink and lost track of time? That would have to do. Resignedly, he set the bottle on the counter. He slipped off his shoes and carried them down the long corridor to the master suite. He removed his clothes in the dark and crawled into bed. When Lucia didn't stir, he knew she was awake, but pretending to be asleep. He turned over on his side, away from her, and tried to quell his thoughts.

Saturday was not a good day. Lucia was quiet, and never asked Michel where he had been. It was almost as if she assumed the worst, and chose not to ask. No fighting, no talking. It was the Saturday before his new job began and it should have been a fun family day, but instead Lucia took the boys to the history museum. Klara stayed home with Bruno, and Michel stayed in bed until noon.

He stood at the window, looking out over the lake, at the mountains in the distance. So much beauty surrounding him and he felt nothing but remorse. *This can't continue*, he told himself. He needed to mend his marriage before anything else. Before the job, before the money. On Monday, he would speak with Gamil. If Gamil fired him, so be it. He would make it clear that there would be no more outings with Farid.

Chapter Fourteen

Gary was happier than he'd been in a very long time. He hadn't realized how miserable he was in New York until he moved to Austria and started teaching in Innsbruck. His exuberance was contagious, and the students loved him. As much as he had enjoyed teaching German, he found that *speaking* German, and teaching American English to the students, was an incredibly rewarding experience. Many of these students wanted to work in America, and were engineering or medical students. Their conversational skills were passable, but all had improved in just a few weeks.

"Bernie, they're so earnest! They're like sponges, absorbing as much as they can. They never want the class to end. A couple of the students approached me about getting together one evening a week, in a casual setting, just talking. They want to practice!"

"Look at you. You're like a kid at Christmas," Bernie said, grinning. She reached out to run her hand through Gary's hair and he pulled her down to sit on his lap. "Or maybe I'm the kid and you're

Santa," she added with a laugh.

"One of them suggested a weekly meeting at someone's house. You know, each week one of us hosts a casual supper. What do you think?"

Bernie shrugged as she considered. "I guess we could do that. We could probably fit six more bodies in here. But holding a session in a café would be easier, don't you think?"

"Maybe. I just think the students are comfortable in a house. And it would go a long way toward my relationship with them. I won't agree to it, though, if you don't want to."

Bernie wrapped her arms around his neck. "No, I'm on board. It's fine. I love seeing you so happy."

He took off his glasses. "Everything is the way it should be. I can't imagine life being any better." He pulled her close and felt the heat of her body.

***

Karl Berset woke up and realized he could stay in bed. It was the first day of his retirement, just like being on vacation, but a long vacation without end. He lay very still and focused on different parts of his body, as he'd read an article about it recently. First his toes, then his feet, and so on up his legs. Nothing moved, shook, or twitched as he concentrated, and this helped to relax his mind. He recited the alphabet, the days of the week, the twenty-six cantons of Switzerland.

His last day of work had been memorable, for sure. He'd already cleaned out his office, and with the help of a couple of the younger men, one with a car, he brought the important items to his house. He made telephone calls to colleagues he'd come to know over the years, letting them know he'd soon be retired. He trained his replacement, a woman named Mirjan who was all business and found none of his small jokes the least bit funny. Karl was surprised that his legendary charm didn't work with this one, and assumed there must be something wrong with her. He lost track once during a recitation of the Swiss Financial Market Supervisory Authority, but Mirjan picked up immediately and made no comment about his lapse. She knew about his disease, as did nearly everyone in the office, and no one treated him any differently. One of the younger women was especially kind to him, so much so that he'd erupted one day and yelled at her to treat him the way she always had, with disdain and disregard.

"I know I wasn't very well-liked here," he'd said, about two weeks earlier, "so don't change that on my account. Don't do me any favors because I'm sick," he said. Then his pinched face softened and he continued. "See? Maybe I could blame my entire shitty personality on this wretched disease. Then you'd be forced to like me." He waited, stared them down, then burst out laughing. Soon the others were laughing with him, too.

On his last day of work, his co-workers

chipped in to buy sandwiches and cake, and all afternoon it was like a party in the normally quiet bank offices. Karl temporarily forgot his illness. Ella arrived at four o'clock, and chatted with Carmen, the receptionist, while Karl met briefly with the upper management. They exited an office and, in front of Ella and his co-workers, the chairman of the small bank presented Karl with a Breitling watch, engraved on the back with his initials and dates of service. And then it was time to leave. Karl shook hands with each of his co-workers.

"So, that is it," he said quietly to Ella. "Time is up." His eyes danced around the office, taking in the picture and making a mental imprint. He would not be back.

"Walk me home, my love," Ella whispered, taking his arm.

"As long as you remember the way," he countered.

And now, he didn't want to get out of bed. Karl felt as if he could sleep for a month. He turned to his side and pulled the blanket up around his neck. He heard Ella banging around in the kitchen. Perhaps she was making a special breakfast, he thought, his senses wakening to the aroma of coffee.

He felt her hand on his shoulder and rolled onto his back. Squinting at her in the light, he said, "You were making a lot of noise in the kitchen, *cherie*. Did you create something wonderful to eat?"

She inched the blanket down his body.

"You'd better get your lazy bones out of this bed to find out. You may be retired, Karl, but you're not dead."

"Not yet," he shot back, but seeing her face, he grinned and swung his legs around before hoisting himself from the warm bed. "I want us to go somewhere," he said.

"Come eat," she replied, handing him a bathrobe. "Breakfast is ready." He shuffled to the kitchen. As Karl sat, Ella pulled plates from a warm oven and set them on the table.

After breakfast, Karl remained seated at the table, watching Ella wash the morning dishes. He thought he could be very happy with a routine such as this each morning: his wife rousing him from a warm bed to enjoy a lovingly-prepared breakfast.

"But I mean it, Ella. I would like for us to have a trip. While I am still able to travel." He waited.

Ella turned away from the sink, her blonde hair falling over one eye. She raised a soapy hand to brush it away, and Karl rose to stand close to her. "Please, *cherie*. I don't know how much time there is, or for how long I will able to function. Let's go somewhere. Please. You choose." He rested his hands on her hips.

Ella laid her hand against his cheek. Her fingertips were warm and still a little wet. She traced his hairline. "Okay. We'll stop in Geneva to see Dani first. Then south, to France, and Spain. Portugal, maybe? We'll chase the sun, my love."

"Can we leave right now?" His question

made her laugh, which was exactly the reaction he sought. He loved to see her face crinkle up in merriment.

"Let me make some arrangements first! Friday? I'll let Dani know, and research places to stay. This time of year, it shouldn't be hard."

"What about her test?" Karl furrowed his brow. "When is her test?"

"I'll find out. Not yet. Not until springtime. And Jean-Michel? Have you heard from him?"

Karl shook his head. "No, I'm sure the boy has a lot to think about. Perhaps I'll telephone him today. I have nothing else to do." He curled a lock of Ella's hair behind her ear. "And Paul? Has he said anything more?"

Ella shook her head and Karl saw the joy fade from her eyes. Damn, he shouldn't have asked. "We need to give him time, Karl. Listen, why don't you come with me?"

"To the hair salon? The market?" Karl patted his wife's bottom. "My first true day of retirement. I think I'll enjoy it right here," he said.

Once Ella had left the house, Karl returned to his work in progress, the story he'd begun weeks before. He opened his laptop, entered the password to open the document, and stared at the one word he'd typed: *Bernadette.*

Chapter Fifteen

He stared at her name for a long time. Bernadette. Jean-Michel's mother. Would Jean-Michel want to read this? What had Bernadette told him? Karl began to type as the swelling tide of memory engulfed him:

Bernadette Maguire was the last American student I seduced. In September of 1978, she walked into the bank where I worked in Fribourg and stood before me, braless. Of course I noticed. She wanted me to notice. She enticed me, and it worked. Bernadette, however, was different from the other American students. Whereas many of the girls were brazen and self-assured, Bernadette was modest. Standing before me as she did that day, I knew she was self-conscious. Embarrassed, even. I thought at the time that I would not pursue her, even though I found her very attractive. Ella had just informed me that she was pregnant, and we were ecstatic, but she was being very careful, and would not allow me to make love to her, even at three months. The doctor had told us we could enjoy sex almost up to the day she delivered, but Ella said no. She worried about everything with the pregnancy. I was frustrated, of course, and there was young Bernadette, showing me her breasts, their shape visible beneath a thin sweater. And all that red hair – I was intrigued by the girl. But I did not act upon my urges, not then.

It was truly a coincidence that I would see her days later. She and one of her friends entered the Eurotel bar just as I was leaving with some colleagues. Perhaps it was fate, I'm not sure, but I stopped. I stopped, and everything changed after that. We shared some drinks, talked a bit. She was charming in all aspects – intelligent, shy, and seemingly unaware of her sexuality. I asked if she would have dinner with me, and she accepted. Did I want more? Yes. I wanted this girl, even as I knew I'd be breaking a vow I'd made to myself.

Living close to the town of Fribourg, I'd always made sure not to be seen in public with one of the girls. There were eyes and ears everywhere, so I borrowed an apartment from a friend who was away, and in that apartment, I made love to Bernadette. I did not realize that it was her first time until we were at a point where there was no turning back. Being her first lover was a heady experience, as it had been with Ella. There was no other man to whom I would be compared. I took pleasure in exploring Bernadette's body, and to this day I can still recall her creamy skin, her coppery curls, and the sounds she made when I touched her.

She returned to me the following night, but the magic was gone. I realize now that for me, the joy was in the hunt and capture. Ella was visiting her parents in Belgium that weekend, and I didn't want to be alone, so I'd invited Bernadette to return to the apartment. But in my mind, we'd already departed from each other. Besides, I expected not to see her again after that one weekend. In fact, when she left me that morning to meet her friends at church, I ridiculed her. I wanted her to despise me; it was so much easier that way.

Little did I know then that our brief weekend affair would result in a pregnancy. I was focused on Ella, and her pregnancy, and had pretty much put Bernadette from my mind. She came to see me at the bank once or twice, I can't remember the conversation, but it was difficult. She was sweet and honest about her feelings, even though I never believed she really loved me. She didn't know me at all, and if she had, she would have hated me. Finally, knowing I had to do something drastic to get away from her, I asked to be transferred, and began working at the bank in Lausanne.

Ella gave birth to Paul in March of 1979. On Valentine's Day that year, we traveled together to see Dr. Hanna Schmid at the hospital in Fribourg. I recall Ella's beautiful red dress, her luminescence, even at the late stage of her pregnancy. Ella never complained, never showed any discomfort. As we exited the hospital to the waiting taxi, I saw Bernadette Maguire making her way up the hill to the hospital. Now, as I think back, I'm sure that for a split second it crossed my mind that she could be pregnant, but the thought disappeared just as quickly as it had come to me. I wouldn't allow myself to consider the possibility. It was February, and she wore a coat. I couldn't tell she was pregnant, but I did see her. And the look on her face almost did me in. I hurried into the waiting cab and we left. I never looked back. And I managed to banish her from my thoughts. I had a good life with Ella, and we welcomed Paul as any new parents would: with overwhelming joy and adoration.

Six years ago, in 2002, on a late autumn afternoon, Ella answered the door to find two women at our house. One of them was older and remained back from the house at the street. And the other one was Bernadette Maguire. I had come to the door to see who was there, and I recognized her as soon as I saw her face. That hair. Bernadette. My Bernadetta, from so long ago. Ella was confused then, and she left me to speak with Bernadette. I stood outside in the cold and listened as she told me that she had given birth to a child in 1979, my child. It must have been a short time after our Paul was born. She was emotional, I could see, and trying to keep from crying as she spoke. The older woman with her was an aunt, and she explained that they were in Switzerland on vacation. Bernadette wouldn't give me any more information about this child, not even the gender, and after telling me, she left rather abruptly.

I returned inside the house to find Ella seething with anger. She had heard Bernadette tell me about a child. Ella had tolerated my indiscretions over the years, and I am ashamed to admit to three or four dalliances with women during our marriage. But no one had ever had the audacity to show up at our home, and Ella felt violated by the intrusion. We had a loud and furious fight, and I moved out the following day. We were separated, and I blamed Bernadette for my troubles. Of course, I was not yet at a point where I would take responsibility for my own failings. In my mind, it was her fault for showing up, for ruining my marriage. And I wanted very much to find this child she'd birthed.

I contacted my old pal Henri Rutz. Henri was a retired police officer who worked independently as a private investigator. We met, and I relayed my story. He agreed to look for the child, who at that time would have been in his or her young twenties, as the child was born shortly after my son Paul entered the world. Henri conducted inquiries but I still did not have any solid information. All I knew was that the child would have been born in Fribourg, most likely at the same hospital where Ella had given birth to Paul. Henri started there.

He was still working the case when a young woman showed up to the bank one morning and asked to see me. She was a petite girl, very pretty, dark hair and features. I suppose at the time, if I'd taken the time to think about it, I would have realized that she looked nothing like Bernadette or me, that it was improbable for her to be our child based on looks alone. But I wasn't thinking clearly. I brought her to my office for a private conversation. She mentioned Bernadette and I *panicked. I was so sure she had come to me for money. I wanted to shut her up, to keep her away from my family. I wanted my Ella back. In an attempt to get rid of her, I gave her an envelope of money. A lot of money. I'd had it in a locked drawer in my desk; since Ella had kicked me out, I'd squirreled away some cash in case we divorced and I lost everything. I handed this girl an envelope containing thirty thousand francs and she left. It was only later that I learned from Henri that she was not my child. At that time, I had no idea who this girl was, but the realization that I'd just handed over thirty thousand francs to a stranger brought on severe chest pains. I had a heart attack and landed in the hospital.*

For a long time thereafter, I harbored ill feelings toward Bernadette Maguire, as I continued to believe that she was the cause of my pain and suffering. But it wasn't Bernadette, of course. I was the one who controlled my life. I made bad decisions. I cheated on my wife. The fact that Ella was even willing to speak with me was a gift. After my heart attack, she visited and we talked for hours. I confessed to her, and in so doing, I began to be honest with myself. We have since mended our marriage, and every day I am grateful for her.

And this brings me to the present day. I have been diagnosed with Huntington's Disease, which causes a progressive breakdown of nerve cells in my brain. I inherited the disease, and I have passed along the risk to Paul, to Dani, and to my son by Bernadette, who is named Jean-Michel. At the time of this writing, I've developed some of the symptoms: involuntary twitches, short-term memory loss, insomnia, fatigue, and a lack of impulse control that can result in outbursts. Sometimes I act without thinking. Sexual promiscuity is another symptom, but I haven't done that in years. Let's hope it doesn't start up again. Poor joke there. My Ella is an angel. She could leave me with good reason. I've been a rotten husband, unworthy of her love and forgiveness, but she stays.

My son Paul and I have argued for years. Although he believes me to be disappointed in him, I am not. I admire his independence and unwillingness to go along with everyone else. I suppose I'm envious of him in a way. I do worry, though. Paul and his wife Sophie are expecting a child. He does not want to take the test that will determine if he carries the Huntington's gene. He doesn't want to know. When I do pray, I pray for Paul.

My darling daughter Daniele, Dani, who lives in Geneva and works as a model, will have the test. She wants to know. I would, however, like to see Dani marry soon and settle down with a man who is able to care for her. Having the Huntington's gene doesn't mean one will develop the disease immediately; look at me, I wasn't aware of it until recently, and I am sixty years old. My heart would break for my lovely Dani, though, and I pray she is spared.

Jean-Michel showed up at our door recently, although I wasn't surprised to finally meet my son.

I had contacted Bernadette when I first found out, and asked her to please contact Jean-Michel. He is a fine young man who looks very much like his mother. He is married with two sons, and I do hope he chooses to be tested. Of course, I wish that the odds favor all three of my children, but I am realistic enough to know that at least one of them may end up marked for the difficult future that awaits their father.

I did not live a life of goodness and integrity. I betrayed my wife and I betrayed the young girls who believed the lies I told them in order to fulfill my carnal desires. I hide the scars of rancor and remorse. For these transgressions, I am truly regretful and I hope that those I hurt will forgive me for being a very flawed human being.

Karl Berset, 2 fevrier 2009

Chapter Sixteen

Into his second month, Michel felt he had hit his stride at work. And he believed the matter involving Farid was behind him. At the end of his first day of work in early January, he'd stated to Gamil that he wasn't interested in going out with Farid anymore.

"I'm very happily married, Gamil. My family responsibilities begin when I leave my job, and I'm simply not interested in going out at night, unless the purpose is strictly business-related."

Gamil had leaned back in his big chair and used his thumb and index finger to stroke the trim black beard on his chin. He surveyed Michel with flinty black eyes.

"So you tell Farid then. Why is this a problem?"

Michel shifted in his chair. "Perhaps that was my misunderstanding then, and I apologize. I thought perhaps the social aspect was expected of me."

"Jean-Michel, we value family very much. And we want you to be a happy employee. Certainly I don't want you to have strife in your marriage. By all means, you should let Farid know that you no longer will join him in the evening." Gamil rocked in his chair and continued to gaze at Michel.

Michel attempted to smile but his face was tight. Instead he nodded. "Thank you, sir. I appreciate your opinion." He stood. "I'll see you tomorrow."

"You had a good first day of work. Go home to your family," Gamil said, steepling his fingers under his chin.

Michel had made a quick exit. Once he'd arrived home, he pulled Lucia away from the kitchen. The boys were in the wing with Klara.

"Lulu, sit with me for a minute," he said, pulling her down next to him. Lucia was quiet but waited.

"I know we have made an adjustment moving here, and everything is still very new. I've been on edge these past few days, and I'm sorry. The pressure of the new job was weighing on me heavily. I also owe you an explanation about last Friday night."

"I'm listening," she said, folding her hands in her lap. She cast her eyes down and sat very still.

"Gamil's brother Farid? You remember, from New Year's Eve in the city?" She nodded, and raised her eyes to him. He looked deep into them - light blue eyes that were wide and trusting. *Oh, Lucia*, Michel thought, *how could I ever hurt you?* "The first time Farid invited me out, I was under the impression that it was part of the job. You know, because he is Gamil's brother. It was when I was here from Fribourg, remember? When I was interviewed for the job. Gamil mentioned his brother and something about listening to jazz music. So I thought that's where we were going, but they took me to a club, a private men's club, and they brought women in. One woman just for me." He felt Lucia stiffen next to him, but she said nothing. He laid his big hand over her two small ones, still clasped together in her lap.

"Nothing happened, Lulu, nothing at all. You know I would never do anything like that," he said. "Look in my eyes, *amore*."

"Was she very pretty, this woman?" Lucia's voice was so small, Michel almost didn't hear her.

"She was nothing like you, *amore*. Very skinny, very hard. Too much makeup." He met her eyes. "No, Lulu, not pretty." He took a breath. He had to be honest with her. "I think she was very sad. I went with her to a private room, but I told her straight away that nothing would happen. Nothing, Lulu. I drank a bottle of water. She looked almost relieved that I didn't want to engage her. I think she is an expensive prostitute, and perhaps she works for Farid, or one of his friends."

"Oh dear," Lucia said.

"Anyway, she said she would never tell Farid, and that she had already been paid for the evening. Like Farid was giving me a gift or something." Michel shook his head.

Lucia gently pulled her hands away from his. "And Michel, last Friday evening?"

Michel straightened his spine. "Yes, Lulu. It was Farid again. The messenger who brought the envelope? It was an invitation to join him. I tried to find Gamil at the hotel. Lulu, I hadn't even started work yet! I felt I must speak to Gamil. I would tell him that if I had to go out with Farid to keep my job, then I would quit." He looked up to see her large eyes. "It's true! I would quit the job if it meant I had to do that, because I did not like the implication. Look, I would never break my vow to you, but the situation made me uncomfortable. Anyway, I couldn't reach Gamil. He was in Italy, in meetings. My short training last Friday afternoon was just nothing. And Gamil never returned my phone call, so, yes, I did go out. And I'm so sorry I didn't tell you. I was still worried that if I didn't, I could lose the job I hadn't even begun yet." Michel paused. "It all sounds silly when I say it out loud. But we've invested everything in this job."

"And the woman from the club?"

"Yes, she was there again. And again I went to the room with her. All so Farid would think nothing was different. We talked. Only talked. No drinking, no touching, nothing." He flashed back to Dani unbuttoning his shirt and shut his eyes, afraid Lucia might see the lie hidden there. "I fell asleep on the sofa, and when I woke, she was gone. I left the building, found a taxi, and came home."

"And that's all, Michel?" She peeked up at him through her long lashes.

He gulped and nodded. "After my first day

of work, I went straight to Gamil's office and told him. I told him that I wasn't comfortable going out with Farid, that I had no interest in this club. I said that when my work was done at the hotel, I would return home to my family. I would only attend a social event if it was related to business with the hotel."

"And what did he say?"

"Not a lot, actually. He said that I should simply tell Farid I'm not interested in accompanying him to the club. So I did. I had his number, and I called him, and told him that I wouldn't be going out anymore."

"And he was okay with this?"

"Apparently so." Michel fell silent. Farid had peppered Michel with sharp questions. *Was he disappointed in Dani? Did she not please him? Would she not agree to do things?* He'd find another girl for him. No, no, Michel had nearly shouted back, there was nothing wrong with Dani. He reiterated that he was happily married, and he was sure he heard Farid laugh at the other end of the phone, but he simply replied, "Okay, Jean-Michel, if that is what you want," and ended the call.

Lucia had nodded and said she understood. Said she actually felt sorry for this girl Dani. And after that day, in the first week of January, everything had been okay. Michel worked hard, and when he arrived home in the evening, Lucia had supper waiting. The boys were clean and well-behaved, most of the time. His mother seemed better, too, with Bruno having Ahmed to assist him. Farid had not contacted him, and Gamil had not spoken of him. Michel didn't even know if Farid was still in Geneva.

Occasionally he thought of Dani, but only to worry for her well-being. He knew nothing of her relationship with Farid, but Michel thought the man was crass and rough. He hoped Dani was not mistreated by him. Either way, he would not see her again.

Since then, he'd been concentrating on work, doing the best job he could, and returning home in the evening. Gamil seemed to be pleased with his job performance. Michel loved the hotel. It was a faster-paced environment than working in Fribourg. Two nights ago he welcomed a famed violinist from America, who performed at Victoria Hall to sold-out crowds. The crown prince of a lesser-known African country was expected to arrive over the weekend, and there were plenty of weddings booked well into the summer.

He had met twice with the genetic counselor, and had not changed his mind about having the test. He needed to know, so he could prepare himself and Lucia for an uncertain future. Whatever the outcome, he would ensure that his family was secure.

On a Thursday evening in early February, he walked into his house and heard Lucia's sobs. He left his coat and shoes at the door and rushed into the kitchen.

"Lulu, what is it? What happened?"

She turned to him, her hands covered with

bits of ground beef and egg, her eyes red and puffy.

"Papa's nurse quit! He just left! Said he wouldn't do the job anymore, and now he's gone. Mama is crying, she is so upset. How could he just leave?"

"I'll be right back," he said, and jogged down the long corridor to get to the other side of the massive house.

Michel opened the French doors and ran shoeless under the portico, where another set of doors awaited him. He flung them open and ran to his parents' bedroom, where he found his mother feeding his father. Bruno stared ahead, with not a flicker of recognition in his vacant eyes.

"Mama," he said, coming to her side. Klara's face was calm. Michel knew she wouldn't cry in front of her husband, she'd stated that previously. She believed it would upset him, although Michel thought that at this point, his father wouldn't know the difference.

"What happened, Mama?" He laid his hand on her arm, and she set down the spoon. She stood and took Michel's arm, leading him away from Bruno. With a glance back, she gripped his arm.

"That man! He told me he was tired of the job. He didn't want to do it anymore. Can you believe it? He said Bruno was difficult! Look at your father, Michel. He's just like a baby, passive, complacent. He doesn't thrash about, he doesn't resist." She shook her head with disdain and

Michel could see the tension set in again. He put his arm around her thin shoulders.

"Okay, we'll find someone else, Mama. It may take a few days, but we'll find someone else." Silently, he wondered what had happened. What would make Ahmed quit so suddenly? "Come on, I'll help you. You finish feeding him. I'll prepare the bathing items. Then you go and eat supper with Lucia and the boys. I'll stay here. Tell Lulu to keep a plate warm for me." He kissed his mother's cheek and withdrew to the large bathroom adjacent to his parents' bedroom.

Bruno was usually bathed in his bed now, as it was too difficult to bring him to the tub or shower. Michel rolled up his sleeves. He found a large basin and filled it with warm water, then took a clean cloth from several piled next to the sink. He squeezed some liquid soap into the water and swished it around, then returned to the bedroom. Klara had moved the food items out of the way: bowl, cup, utensils, napkins. Together they worked to undress Bruno and position him. All his life, Michel had thought of his father as burly, strong, but now he was thin and frail.

Klara was the first to gasp when she saw him. "Michel! Oh my God, look!"

Michel caught his breath when he saw the bedsores on his father's back, and on his buttocks and legs as well. Klara sobbed as Michel turned his father to his side, propping him up with pillows so he wouldn't fall back.

"He needs to be seen by a doctor. Perhaps

the hospital, Mama."

Klara nodded dumbly. Michel picked up the phone and dialed.

***

The first gathering of Gary's students was in just two hours, and he'd called Bernie at the apartment. She was cleaning and laughed that he was interrupting her.

"Don't worry about it, love. They won't care."

"I just have to wipe up the bathroom," she said. "I don't want your students to think we live like slobs."

Gary chortled. "Well, we don't! Really, don't worry. Everything will be great."

"I'm leaving in a few minutes to pick up the food from the market. A little of everything, so they can choose what they like. What about drinks?"

"They all bring beer and wine, that's the arrangement. Just make sure we have soft drinks available. Bernie, if you want to wait until I get home, I'll stop at the market."

"I'm heading there now, love. Everything else is fine."

"Okay, just be careful," Gary said. "I was nearly run over by a speeding ambulance the other day." The hospital was situated just past the university, and he'd grown accustomed to the constant sirens wailing past him when he walked to and from work.

When Gary arrived home, he saw that Bernie had arranged the furniture in a little circle, with the chairs from the dining table set across from the sofa and chairs. A couple of large pillows sat on the floor. He had seven in his class, so there would be nine in total.

He was about to jump in the shower, but when he saw how pristine the bathroom was, he figured he'd better not risk messing it up.

"I'm back!" He heard Bernie at the front door and met her, taking the cloth bags from her hands. "Honey, the place looks great." He hoisted the heavy bags to the counter and peeked inside.

"There's a little bit of everything," she said, unpacking cheeses and olives and slices of meat. "I'll lay everything out here so your students can help themselves."

Gary looked around. The apartment was all set. She'd taken care of everything. That was his Bernadette. Gary smiled and grabbed a bottle of beer from the refrigerator. He unscrewed the top and tossed it in the trash can. He watched Bernie arrange the food on platters. It was like art, he thought. Only his wife could make salami and pickles look so pretty.

The doorbell rang. Gary opened the door to four of his students, who burst into the apartment full of energy and laughter. They shrugged out of parkas and boots, and padded into the living room on sock-clad feet, their faces flushed. Bernie took their coats and piled them on the bed.

One of his students, Greta, watched Bernie

disappear into the bedroom and turned back to Gary. "You lay our coats on your bed?"

"Sure," Gary said. He laughed and turned his palms up. "We don't have a coatroom," he chuckled.

"I bring beer and so does Anders," said Herman, lifting a six-pack of Stiegl beer. Anders, tall and thin, with blond hair like straw, held a six-pack in each hand.

"Plenty of beer!"

"Stiegl? That's new to me." Gary plucked a bottle from the carton and held it up to inspect.

"You will like this, Professor Baptista. Austria has had Stiegl for over five hundred years." Herman glanced at his friend Martin, who nodded vigorously behind thick eyeglasses.

Bernie walked out of the bedroom just as the doorbell rang again. She opened the door to three women, each of whom lifted a bottle of wine. "Hello!" they chimed in unison. Bernie smiled and opened the door wide. They shook snow from their hair and clomped their boots on the doormat before entering.

"Hi, I'm Gary's wife, Bernadette," she said, offering her hand.

Gary stepped forward and accepted the coats. "Bernie, this is the rest of my group: Annie, Franziska, Miriam. Ladies, your friends are in there."

"Honey, give me those," Bernie said, taking the heavy coats in her arms. "Go and join the group. I'll be around, but then I may take a walk and leave you with your students."

"No! Stay, Bernie. You don't have to leave. You'd probably add a lot to the discussion."

"This is your class, honey." She gave him a quick peck on the cheek before steering him toward his group. "I'll see you in a bit."

Gary watched her slip out through the door. It wasn't like Bernie to be antisocial, but she did say she wanted him to enjoy the evening. She probably just went to the café down the street, he thought, and turned back to the seven faces surrounding him. His students were munching on food and sipping beer or wine, chatting in their self-conscious English. He wished Bernie had stayed – she could have offered a lot to these kids. Well, he thought, it's cold outside. She won't last long. He turned back to the students and asked them what they thought about Roger Federer's defeat at the Australian Open.

***

Bernie stepped into the warmth of the café and pulled off her parka. She hung it on an iron hook next to the door and found a table by the window. She ordered hot tea and felt a rumbling in her stomach. And with all that food back in the apartment, she thought wryly. When the waitress brought tea, she asked for a bowl of soup and some bread. Bernie poured steaming tea from a bright red teapot and warmed her hands around the mug.

Where do I fit in here, she thought. *Gary and I have been in Innsbruck for over a month, and still, I don't know what I'm doing.* If she was going to teach, she should teach. She hadn't done a thing to find out about the possibility, not even one inquiry. She wasn't going to practice law here. So what then? She pulled a notebook from her bag and opened it to a blank page. It beckoned, this rectangle of white, begging to be written on. Maybe a journal about this year in Austria. A blog. *I should have brought my laptop,* she thought, *but I was in such a hurry to leave.* A blog. Sure, why not. And maybe more, perhaps a book, or a collection of stories. She fished around in her bag for a pen and began writing down everything she remembered from the first month – notes, snippets, a description of their apartment. The area surrounding them, New Year's Eve, the food. Everything she could think of. When the soup arrived, she took a break to eat, then quickly returned to writing. Bernie wrote as fast as she could. Incomplete sentences, she didn't care. She just wrote and wrote, filling one page after another.

She was so consumed with writing that she nearly screamed when she felt a hand on her shoulder. "Gary! What are you doing here? What time is it?"

Gary scraped a wooden chair across the floor and sat beside her. "The group broke up an hour ago, and I started to worry. I came here first. Bernie, you didn't have to leave us. I missed you." He pushed his glasses up the bridge of his nose, red now from the cold.

"I just felt that you should have your group

without me. I'm sure I'll see them all again, and they were great. They really look up to you, you know." Bernie sandwiched his cold hands between hers. "Where are your gloves?" She signaled to the waitress for more tea.

"There's plenty of food at home, you know," he said with a wink.

"Gary, I came here to think. Tried to figure out what it is I'm going to do while we're here. And the first thing I'm going to do is write. I think I'd like to start a blog. I should have started it last month when we first arrived, but I'll catch up. I've been writing down everything I remember, and I'll start tomorrow. Even if no one ever reads it, that's okay. Well, Joanie will read it, and my aunt Joan. Who knows? Maybe there's a book in me, too." She grinned at him. "But tell me how it went tonight."

The waitress replaced the empty teapot with another one, larger. Gary laid his hands against the warm surface before filling their mugs.

"It was good! A couple of the students have a better handle on American English – two of them have been to the states – but everyone seemed eager to learn, and we're looking forward to the next meeting. By the way, they all wanted me to let you know that you're welcome at these sessions." He raised the mug to his face, where the steam fogged his glasses.

"Maybe next time, honey. I wanted this one to be just you and your protégées." She packed away the notebook and pen. "We'll have our tea and head back home. What time is it, anyway?"

"Almost ten-thirty," Gary said, looking at his watch. They finished their tea, donned heavy coats again, and Bernie left money on the table, nodding at the waitress, who was making her way to the table. "All set," she said, knowing that she didn't need to leave a tip but leaving extra anyway.

***

That didn't take long, Karl mused over coffee. Ella, true to her word, had consulted with their travel agent and booked a trip. She hated to fly, so it was agreed they would travel by train. First stop: Geneva, where they would meet Dani for dinner and stay overnight. The following morning, after breakfast, it was on to Lyon, France, then an overnight train to Lisbon. Ella had booked a comfortable sleeping compartment, and an excellent hotel in Lisbon. "It was highly recommended by the travel agent," she said.

"Did you call Dani?" Karl asked. He drummed his fingers on the table in an irregular, awkward beat.

"Yes, she can meet us, but she said it has to be early. She has a late photo shoot tonight," Ella said as she folded clothes. The weather in Lisbon in February would be milder, but not summery. She laid folded layers of light clothing in their suitcase and closed the zipper around its perimeter.

"Perhaps we could watch this photo shoot? I would love to see my Dani in her element," he murmured.

"We can ask her, *cheri*, but I don't know. She said she will meet us at the hotel. I have everything for our trip in this bag." She lowered the larger rolling suitcase to the floor and rolled it to stand sentry by the door. "And the essentials – toiletries, pajamas. and a change of clothes, here." She zipped up a smaller bag and placed it on the floor next to the larger one.

"Have you spoken with Paul?"

"Yes, he knows our itinerary, I recited it to him. We all have our phones with us anyway," Ella said. "Come on, let's get going. I called for a taxi to the station." She slipped into a light coat and helped Karl do the same.

"I'm glad I have my sweater, Ella darling. This is a coat meant for May, not November," Karl said.

"It's February, and you won't want a heavy coat in Lisbon, *cheri*. Come."

"February. That's what I meant," Karl mumbled.

They arrived at the Geneva train station and stepped onto the platform. Back in Lausanne, Ella had arranged for their luggage to be delivered to the hotel. She knew Karl could not handle one of the bags, and she alone couldn't manage both. They walked, arm in arm, past men and women, old and young, wrapped in wool, hurrying to a new destination.

The hotel was situated at the edge of the

lake, and Karl hailed a taxi. They wore clothing more suited to a warm spring day, and it was cold in the open air.

Karl and Ella walked up to the front desk and Karl saw a flash of orange hair as he turned. Before he could see who owned the orange hair, it was gone.

"I swear I just saw Jean-Michel back there," he said. "When he came to visit us in December, didn't he say he was in Geneva?" Karl frowned, trying to recall the conversation. He hadn't heard from Jean-Michel since that visit, just before Christmas. He thought about him often, and wondered if he should contact him.

"I think he said he had *been* in Geneva, Karl, but I don't know if he said he lived there. I think he lives in Fribourg."

"Yes, yes, of course. Odd, though, it really looked like him." Karl twisted his body in an effort to maybe see the young man again. "Perhaps I'm now hallucinating."

"Stop," she whispered, patting his arm. She turned to the front desk clerk, who typed on his computer and handed her a plastic card to enter their room. "Thank you," she said to the clerk, and took her husband by the arm. "Come, let's see the room and relax before we meet Dani."

They walked together to a bank of elevators. When the doors parted, they stepped inside and Ella pushed number six. And just before the doors closed, Karl saw him again. That was definitely Jean-Michel. But he didn't say anything to Ella. She wouldn't believe him, anyway.

Chapter Seventeen

Bernie had found a new purpose and restored energy writing her blog. Hanna sent an email inviting her and Gary to Fribourg for the weekend, but she begged off. Gary was busy, even on the weekends. And Bernie wanted to save their next trip for Geneva, to see Michael. She'd sent him a text and he'd replied that yes, he and Lucia would love to see her. It was a long trip, though, and one she didn't want to make without Gary. She'd have to wait until his work load eased up; perhaps during the spring vacation in March.

Meanwhile, Gary was exuberantly happy. He spoke German all day long, and sometimes lapsed back into it at home. It only reminded Bernie that she hadn't made any effort to learn German, and that frustrated her. German was hard! French was so easy in comparison. Even Italian wasn't difficult, but German! She considered signing up for a class at the university; with Gary as a visiting professor, she could get a discount. Not that money was tight, but life was different these days. Bernie had no income; all of their money came from Gary, and she didn't like it. It made her feel dependent, something she wasn't used to at all. Perhaps she should offer her services as a tutor. She could post notices at the university.

She finished her blog post and saved the document, then typed up a notice for tutoring, and added her contact information. She printed out one sheet. It looked good, and she knew there was a copy shop on the way to the university. She'd have copies made, and would post them around, maybe drop some at the library. *Great*, she thought, *progress. Let's do this.*

She glanced out the window at the drizzle, turning the snow to mush. The sky was heavy, the pavement black. Holiday decorations were down, and spring seemed far away. This time of the year was depressing, Bernie thought. No wonder people liked to vacation to warmer places right about now. There was no new life yet, and she felt as if she was in a holding pattern. She hated it. Maybe they *should* go to Geneva this weekend. It wouldn't be any warmer, but at least it would offer something different. And it would be so enjoyable to see Michael and his family.

She pulled on rubber boots, bright green ones Gary found for her last week, and slipped into her raincoat. She placed the tutor notice in a flat folder and tucked it inside her waterproof bag, and grabbed her umbrella from the stand by the door. She'd make her copies, then find Gary, maybe take him to lunch. Perhaps she could persuade him to take the weekend off. If he agreed, she'd call Michael and make arrangements. She wanted to find out more about the genetic testing, too. He'd let her know that he wanted to have the test, but he'd indicated that it probably wouldn't happen until the spring.

Bernie walked up the road that led to the university, splashing through puddles like a kid. An ambulance sped by, its siren shrill and unnerving. She watched the vehicle grow smaller and disappear into the fog as she turned her face up to catch the rain.

As she approached the university campus, she saw the ambulance again. Two orderlies ran into the building where Gary held his class. Bernie felt a weight in her stomach, as if all of her organs had dropped suddenly. She walked faster, in boots that felt like lead, and approached the building. Just to be sure, she told herself. He'll think I'm nuts, but just to be sure. Where was his classroom? She didn't know, so she ran up the stairs and began looking in every doorway. At the end of the hall, there was a commotion and she ran toward the group of students and professors.

"Gary?" The group parted, just like in the movies, allowing her in. She froze at the doorway when she saw him. Gary lay on the floor, surrounded by the two medical technicians, one of whom strapped an oxygen mask to his face. His eyes were closed.

She was sure she screamed something

before losing consciousness.

***

Ella was in the hotel room's bathroom when the telephone rang. Karl lay supine on the bed, and reached over to the other side to answer it, knocking the receiver to the floor.

"Wait!" he yelled, and rolled off the bed to get to the other side. He picked the receiver up and held it to his ear.

"Dani?"

"Papa, what are you doing? Are you okay?"

"Yes, fine. We're here in the room. Where are you? In the lobby?"

"I'm on my way now. Come down to the lobby and I should be there in just a few minutes."

"Okay," Karl said and replaced the receiver in its cradle. "Ella," he called, knocking on the door. "Come now, we have to meet Dani."

Ella emerged from the bathroom looking radiant. She still took Karl's breath away, after all these years. Karl knew that she'd put an extra effort into her appearance, especially because Dani would be perfectly coiffed and dressed. He didn't want her to think it was a wasted effort.

Karl took his wife's hands in his. "You couldn't look any more beautiful, *cherie*. What a lucky man I am." He leaned to kiss her cheek. Ella glowed.

"Well," she began, looking down at her feet, "I'm no match for our daughter, the high-fashion queen."

"Nor should you be. She is young," and as soon as the words were out, he wished he could pluck them from the air and stuff them in his mouth. He shook his head and raised his palm. "You are not old! You are elegant and classy. Okay?" He tilted his head at her and waited. When he heard her laugh, his chest relaxed.

"Okay, okay, let's go." She picked up her purse as Karl wrapped a soft cashmere shawl around her shoulders.

They took the elevator to the hotel lobby, where crystal chandeliers sparkled and polished floors gleamed. Fresh flowers in tall brass vases adorned tables along mirrored walls. People milled about, crossing this way and that, some in more of a hurry than others. Karl took Ella's elbow and led her gently to a love seat along one wall, where they sat and waited for Dani.

"There she is," he said, when he spied his daughter walk through the revolving door. She looked so tiny, he thought, even in high-heeled boots. Tonight her hair was down, draped over one eye like a glamour girl from the 1940s. She pursed her dark red lips as she glanced around the lobby, but broke into a wide grin as soon as she spotted her parents. They rose and met her halfway, opening their arms to her.

"Papa! Mama," she said, allowing each of her parents to embrace her. When she stepped back from her mother's hug, Ella commented on her hair. "So chic!" she said, and used her index finger to sweep back the tresses that covered her left eye. Then a gasp, for Dani could not completely cover the black eye. Even with all her makeup, it was obvious. Karl's jaw dropped.

"What happened? Dani, you've been hurt?!" Ella's hand flew to her mouth.

Karl tensed. "Did someone do this to you? Who is he?" His voice was angry and too loud. Dani tried to shush him with her hand.

"Please, Papa, keep your voice down! No one did this, don't be ridiculous. I had a slight accident on the set during a photo shoot a few days ago. Too many props, too bright lights, and you know I am a klutz," she said, laughing. She looked them both in the eyes. "Stop it with the faces! I'm fine. Come on, let's go. I'm starving." She walked ahead of them toward the door, as Karl and Ella exchanged a glance.

In the taxi, she asked, "How is the hotel? Everything is all right?"

"It's fine," said Ella, still staring at her daughter. "Papa likes the bed."

"Funniest thing," Karl said, leaning forward. "I could have sworn I saw your brother in the hotel."

"What? Why would Paul be in Geneva?" She frowned at her father, then looked down at his foot, tapping against the cab's door.

"No, not Paul. Your other brother. The one you haven't met yet."

"Well, I want to meet him!" Dani said. "After you return from vacation, let's please plan a day when everyone comes together. Please, Mama?" Her dark eyes locked onto Ella's, and Ella patted her daughter's hand.

"Of course we will. Perhaps after the testing? Have you scheduled yours yet, Dani?"

Dani ran her hands along the tops of her thighs, smoothing down her skirt. Its hem ended just above the knee. "I've just been so busy lately. I haven't even had time to meet with the counselor," she replied in a soft voice. She continued to smooth the leather skirt.

"Are you having second thoughts?" Karl looped his arm through hers. "It's understandable, if you are." He clutched her hand, so small in his. Whatever he could do to protect his little girl, he would find a way to do it. *Please God, just spare her. Give all of it to me, but spare her, I beg you.*

"No, I want to do it. I want to know. I *need* to know. But I just don't have the time right now." She bent her head and let her hair veil her face. Karl looked over at Ella, who shook her head silently.

"Dani, you remember meeting my lawyer, Raphael Klug?" He could see the restaurant up ahead, its lights like beacons.

"I think so." Dani nodded hesitantly.

"He has a brother, Darek. Thirty years old, very successful." He took her hand. "Very good-looking. I think you should meet him."

The taxi stopped in front of Restaurant Gaya.

"Papa, are you trying to fix me up on a date?" Her eyes, shiny with unspilled tears, sparkled from the restaurant lights and Karl thought his heart might burst from love.

He felt the heat rise from his neck to his forehead as he stepped into the cold evening air. "I just think you might like him." He looked at Dani and saw that her eyes were filled again, tears ready to spill over onto her pretty cheeks. "Oh, *cherie*! Forgive me! I didn't mean to upset you." He pulled her to him.

Her voice was muffled against his chest. "It's okay, Papa." She pulled back enough to turn her face up to his. Her hair fell over the bruised eye. "It's okay. Sure, I would like to meet him. Tell him to call me anytime." She reached behind her for her mother's hand and the three of them trooped into the restaurant.

***

Bernie watched the light fade from the sky. Light gray gave way to dark gray, which gave way to black. She wanted to banish the sun, anyway. It had no business shining in her life, on her face. Cold and dark were suitable. But the clock continued to tick, in defiance of her insistence that everything stop. How could life continue? She heard people down the corridor, enjoying a joke. How dare people laugh?

The doctor said cerebral aneurysm. *Thank God he spoke English*, she thought, *or I wouldn't have understood a word*. She was still at the hospital, slumped in a chair in a quiet corner reserved for bereaved family members. Gary was gone, died in the ambulance en route to the hospital. She needed to figure out what to do next. She didn't know his students; had only met them when they came to the apartment. Bernie blinked and realized that was just last night. It seemed so long ago now. Perhaps their numbers were in his cell phone. She touched the white plastic bag that held his phone, wallet, keys.

She'd have to call Gary's children later today. Gary and she had never talked about final wishes. Hell, they were only fifty years old. If Bernie could decide by herself, she'd have him cremated, and take his ashes up to Schwarzsee, their special place. But she had to call Justin and Nicole first. And if they wanted a service back home in America, well, then she'd have to go along with that. *Oh God, how?* She rubbed her face until it hurt. *I'll call Hanna. Hanna will know what to do.*

Bernie remembered telling people the story about her dad, how he died when she was a student in Fribourg. A massive heart attack that took him one spring morning. She recalled saying that, as much as she missed her father every day, wasn't it a better way to go? No suffering, no pain, no long, drawn-out march to death. She bowed her head and wondered if she'd ever be able to speak that way about her husband.

They wouldn't hold the body forever. She looked at her watch. It was nearly six in the evening, meaning it was around noon in America. She pulled out her phone and scrolled through her contacts until she landed on Justin. With a silent prayer, she touched the name and listened as the phone rang. He picked up on the third ring.

"Hey, Bernadette!" Justin's clear, wide-awake voice greeted her. She wondered what kind of a pleasant day she was about to ruin.

"Hey, Jus," she whispered, willing herself not to crack before she could tell him. "Justin. Sit down. This isn't good."

"My dad?" His voice was hoarse.

"Yeah, baby. He collapsed today while he was teaching class. The doctor said he had a brain aneurysm. He died in an instant, honey. There was no pain." She waited for him to digest the words and sucked air into her lungs.

There was silence for a long time, and she imagined he might be gulping air as well. "Okay. Okay." She heard him take a breath. "Wow. Um, I don't even have words right now. Are you coming home? Are you okay, Bernie?"

"I'll do whatever you and Nicole want, sweetheart. If you want me to bring him back, I will. I'll make all the arrangements."

"Um, okay. Let me, uh..." His voice trailed off and she heard his choking sob, just as if he was sitting next to her and not four thousand miles across the ocean.

"Honey, you don't need to decide this instant. Do you want to talk to Nicole? I called you first. If you want me to call her..."

"No, no, Bernie, I'll call her. And I'll tell my mom. Can I call you later today?"

"Of course. Call anytime, Justin."

"Okay. I'll call you later and let you know." There was a pause. "Bernie? I'm really sorry. I know how much you loved each other."

And that did it. That opened the floodgates.

***

Their train left early, before seven in the morning. Karl and Ella had risen at five while it was still dark and quiet, except for an occasional truck passing by on the streets below. They ate a light breakfast in their room, and were at the train station by six-thirty. It was a long trip by rail, but that was the price to pay for not flying. They'd had a late night with Dani, and spent Saturday visiting the museum in Geneva, as Dani was traveling to Montreux to visit with friends. Karl tired easily, and they'd returned so he could nap in the room before dinner.

Neither of them had discussed their daughter's apparent black eye, but Karl knew that Ella didn't believe Dani's excuse any more than he did. She hadn't mentioned a boyfriend, and was even agreeable to meeting Rafe's brother Darek. Perhaps she was involved with someone and wanted to get out. It was difficult to ask, most likely because he was afraid of what her answer might be.

The taxi driver handed their luggage to a porter and Karl and Ella climbed aboard a train that would take them, eventually, to Lisbon.

"It's too bad we don't have any time in Paris, even for lunch," said Ella. She settled into a comfortable seat in the first-class section and Karl sat facing her.

"We'll dine aboard the train, *cherie*, while Paris sails by," Karl replied with an encouraging smile. Ella looked out the window to the platform, where few people walked past. It was early on a Sunday, and most of Geneva was still asleep. Lisbon was twenty-four hours away. He wished Ella had been willing to fly.

Taking his hand, she whispered, "I worry about Dani."

He squeezed back. "I know. But our girl is strong. She won't put up with anyone who doesn't treat her right." He frowned. "She said she was willing to meet Rafe's brother Darek. He would be good for her. I'd like to see her married." He pulled out his phone to send a text message to Rafe.

"But she's only twenty years old, Karl."

"Yes, but this business. She won't be able to model forever. I want her to have someone who can provide for her. You know, for the future." His voice trailed off as he typed on his small phone. When he finished, he looked out the window at a man sweeping up cigarette butts from the platform.

Ella nodded. "I want to make sure we see her on the way back."

"We will, dear, we will. For now, let's enjoy the ride and our vacation."

Chapter Eighteen

Bernie stood in the airport's arrival area and twisted her hands. The flight carrying Justin and Nicole would be on time, she knew. Neither of them had ever been abroad, and she wanted to do everything she could to put them at ease. They'd decided, with their mother's assent, to join Bernie for the service. Justin had told her that whatever she wanted, they would support. Bernie conveyed to Justin that neither she nor Gary had discussed in detail what their wishes were ("We didn't think we'd have to have this discussion for at least another twenty years," she'd said), but when she asked him if they would support cremation, both of them had agreed.

She knew he was with her now, waiting for his children to appear. At least she believed it. Bernie had taken to sleeping with one of his old shirts, just for the scent. The urn holding his ashes was tucked away in her big bag.

She saw Justin first, his head above the crowd, his hand entwined with his younger sister's. Nicole looked good, Bernie thought, healthier, stronger. Well, except for the puffy eyes and tear-stained cheeks. She opened her arms to embrace them both.

"Did either of you sleep?" she asked. Nicole shook her head and looked away. This poor girl, Bernie thought. She's about the same age I was when I lost my dad. And she never had the chance to say goodbye, just like me.

"I took a pill. It helped a little," Justin said.

"The time difference will feel weird for a day or so. Come this way. Would you like coffee, or something to eat?" There was plenty of time before the train to Fribourg.

"Coffee, sure. Nic? You want something?" Justin turned to his sister, who ran a fist under one eye.

"Just water." She rolled her bag to a small table and sat down heavily, if a hundred-pound girl could sit heavily.

"I've got this," Bernie said. "Justin, sit. I'll get it." She left her bag with them and walked a short distance to the coffee shop counter.

They were here for a week, mostly because it was cheaper that way, but Bernie wasn't sure how she was going to fill the time. Fortunately, Hanna had been with her through everything. She'd come to Innsbruck as soon as Bernie had phoned her, and helped her through all the paperwork and arrangements. She'd even offered her house to them, telling Bernie she would vacate it and stay in a hotel, but Bernie had refused. They'd go to Hanna's for dinner one night, and Bernie imagined the kids would want some alone time. She wished Michael still lived in Fribourg. She'd called him last weekend to let him know about Gary, but from the tone of their conversation she could tell he had a lot on his mind. She didn't even ask about the Huntington's test, or whether he'd spoken with Karl lately. She just let him know about the ceremony and told him they'd be staying at the Eurotel. Michael offered to book them into the Hotel de la Rose, but Bernie couldn't bear to stay there, not without Gary.

She ordered two coffees, three croissants, and picked up three bottles of water. If Nicole wouldn't eat a croissant, Bernie would eat it. At the last minute, she saw a bunch of bananas and grabbed a couple. And two bars of chocolate.

She returned and unloaded everything onto the table, sliding a banana to Nicole with a small smile.

"Thanks," she said in her squeaky voice. She looked down at the banana and sniffled.

Bernie cleared her throat. "This is surreal," she said, not really knowing what to say. "I can't believe it's been a week already. A week and a day. It doesn't seem possible."

"Do you know what you're going to do? I mean, afterwards?" Justin asked, taking a bite from his croissant.

"I haven't even thought about it," Bernie said, tracing her fingertip on the tabletop. "I mean, I can't stay in the apartment in Innsbruck. That went with your dad's job. But I'll have to go back." She looked up. "After the ceremony, we can take the train there if you want. And if you don't want to go, I understand. I'll pack everything up, it's just personal stuff. The furniture belongs with the apartment." Would they want to go to Innsbruck? She hadn't planned on it, and now, she hoped they wouldn't want to. But neither of them said anything.

"How's your mom?" she asked, blowing on her coffee.

"She's okay," Justin said. He glanced at Nicole. "She took it hard." He slid the plate, with one croissant on it, toward Nicole, but she shook her head.

"I don't want it," she whispered. She looked around, wide-eyed, at the shops and food stations inside the airport. Bernie understood, and wondered if Nicole would always remember this day every time she set foot in an airport.

A young man approached the table with red roses. Bernie waved a dismissive hand at him, but he plucked two stems from his basket and laid them on the table.

"Alles Liebe zum Valentinstag!" he said, and waited. Bernie squeezed her eyes shut as it hit her. Valentine's Day.

Justin dug into his pocket for money. He pulled out a ten-dollar bill and handed it to the man. "Just take it and go away, please," he growled, and the young man snatched the bill from Justin's hand and scurried away. "I'm sorry, Bernie."

She shook her head. "I forgot," she murmured. "I truly forgot." She and Gary would have spent a romantic day together, she thought; he'd have woken her with chocolate, and would never have bought red roses. No, he would have scoured the florists for early tulips, knowing how much she loved them. She stole a glance at Nicole, who sat zombie-like, unblinking. We need to keep moving, Bernie told herself.

She took a deep breath. "Well, we can get the next train. It leaves in about a half hour, but we might as well make our way down to the tracks." She pushed back in her chair and stood up, almost knocking over a couple of young people right behind her. One of them reached into a bag he was carrying and pulled out a handful of chocolates wrapped in red and pink foil. He tossed them on their table and grinned. "Happy Valentine's Day!"

Oh good God, Bernie thought. Nicole burst into tears, covering her face with both hands. The guy who'd thrown down the hearts looked frightened. His eyes darted from Nicole to Bernie to Justin. Justin drew the man away from the table, and said something to him that Bernie couldn't hear. But she could figure it out by the look on the young man's face. Justin returned and picked up Nicole's bag as well as his own.

"Let's go," he said. "Where's the damn train?"

"This way." Bernie led them toward the escalator that would take them down to the platform.

***

Michel rose early to make breakfast. He cracked eggs into a big bowl, then whisked them with a little cream and some herbs. He opened the refrigerator door and found a small bit of smoked ham, which he minced, to more evenly distribute it. There were potatoes to peel and shred. Oranges to juice. Coffee to brew. He looked around the kitchen and knew there was something he was forgetting. Ah!

He picked up the telephone and dialed the number for his mother. In just a week, Bruno's physical condition had improved dramatically; he was being cared for in a small facility only ten minutes away by bus. Klara visited daily, but having him away from the house also meant she could finally sleep through the night, uninterrupted.

"*Bonjour*, Mama! Come for breakfast, please. I'm cooking eggs. Yes, an omelet. Everyone, yes. Five minutes, okay, Mama." He hung up and smiled. Anything to bring the family back to normal.

He filled the coffeepot with cold water, measured out coffee and flicked the switch to begin brewing. As he cut oranges in half and squeezed the juice out of them, he thought about Bernadette. Poor Bernadette. She'd telephoned him last Sunday with the sad news about her husband Gary. He felt her pain through the phone line, even as she tried to keep her voice steady. She'd mentioned that Gary's children were flying in, and that there would be a small service in Schwarzsee. That was for tomorrow. He hadn't yet mentioned it to Lucia, unsure if she'd want to go. Bernadette had told Michel they were all welcome, but she was insistent that it wasn't necessary. Still, Michel knew it would mean a lot to her if they were there, and the weather forecast for tomorrow was good. No rain, and maybe Schwarzsee would be clear. He'd checked the train and bus schedules, and if they left early tomorrow morning, they could join her. He would ask Lucia later. After breakfast.

"*Bonjour*, Papa," little Jean-Bernard squeaked as he padded into the kitchen.

"*Bonjour*, *p'tit*," Michel replied. "Is Mama awake? And Luca?"

The little boy rubbed his eyes and shook his head. "Apple juice?"

Michel knew the boys preferred the sweet apple juice to the tart orange, and he poured a small cup for his son. "Drink that here, then go wake them up. I have a nice breakfast for everyone."

Jean-Bernard sipped from his cup. "Nonna!" he cried when Klara appeared. He slid down from his seat and ran to embrace his grandmother, who gathered the little boy in her arms. Michel watched his mother's face glow with love for her grandson, and thought again how lucky they were to be together. Even without Bruno, who wouldn't have recognized anyone anyway. But Bruno was safe now, well cared for. *Thank God.*

Michel and Lucia had started house-hunting, and Lucia found a suitable house near the Botanical Gardens. It was big enough for everyone, and available beginning in April. Michel's position at work remained unchanged, and it seemed as though Gamil Almazi was preoccupied with other matters of the company, enough that he left Michel alone to run the hotel most days. Michel didn't mind, though – he had a good staff of loyal employees who seemed to enjoy working for him and for the hotel. He handled the quirky needs of some of the well-known guests and had already received a job offer from the Marriott, which he promptly turned down.

"Mama, would you please let Lucia know that breakfast is almost ready? She can bring Luca."

"Of course," Klara said. "Come, *cheri*, we go wake up your Mama and Luca now." She took Jean-Bernard by the hand and they walked out of the kitchen, leaving Michel to work on his massive omelet.

After breakfast, Klara insisted on cleaning up, claiming it was good for her to be busy. Michel and Lucia moved out of her way and into the living room.

"*Amore*, tomorrow is the service for Bernadette's husband Gary. In Schwarzsee." He shrugged. "I think perhaps we could all go."

Lucia's light blue eyes searched his. "Do you think she wants all of us there? Is this for spreading his ashes? I don't know about the boys being there for that, Michel. Jean-Bernard will ask questions. What do we say to answer him?"

"I don't want the boys to be witness to that, either. We can tell Bernadette; she'll understand. But it would be a chance for all of us to go together. You know, our family. Mama, too, if she wants. I should be there for Bernadette."

"It will be cold in the mountains. We'd have to leave early." Lucia chewed her lip as she thought about it.

Michel nodded. "I just think she would be happy to see all of us. She's never met Luca, hasn't seen Jean-Bernard since he was a baby. And I don't know if she'll stay in Europe without Gary."

Lucia lowered her eyes. "Okay, we go then. You have the schedules?"

Michel nodded. "You're right, we have to leave early, but we can do it." He took his wife's hands in his. "Thank you, *cherie*. For everything." He leaned in to kiss his wife just as the boys bounded into the room. Jean-Bernard made kissing sounds and laughed.

Each parent grabbed a child and covered their faces with loud kisses, to the boys' utter delight.

This is the right thing to do, Michel thought. He hoped his mother would join them, but either way, he was looking forward to seeing Bernadette, perhaps provide some small comfort to her. And it would take his mind off the test, the genetic test, that loomed.

***

Bernadette had booked two rooms at the Eurotel, figuring the kids might want to share a room the first night. She knew Nicole wouldn't want to bunk in with her. They were exhausted, she could tell, after the two-hour train ride from Zurich, where they both drifted in and out of sleep. They rode an elevator up eight stories and settled into their rooms.

"I know you're both tired, and as much as you want to sleep, it's better to try and stay awake. You'll sleep at night and your bodies will adjust more easily to the time difference. I remember letting myself sleep once and was awake then at two in the morning." She gave them a small smile. "Nothing's open around here after eleven."

Justin tossed his duffel bag onto one of the two double beds. Nicole sat on the other bed, barely causing a movement. "Thanks, Bernie. I just don't feel much like walking around the town right now."

"I understand. Listen, how about we take an hour and meet downstairs in the bar? We'll have an early dinner and then I'll leave you alone for the night. Okay with you, sweetheart?" On impulse, Bernie crossed to Nicole, and knelt on the carpet at the foot of the bed. She's so young, so small, Bernie thought. So lost without her daddy.

"Nicky, I was your age when my dad died. It was sudden, too." Nicole raised her eyes to Bernie's and Bernie felt them searching deep, as if the answers to all her questions lay within the depths. She tentatively reached for Nicole's tiny hands and unclenched the fingers from the fisted balls in her lap. "I do understand, honey."

Nicole's tears slipped down her cheeks and dropped onto her shirt. Bernie found a clean tissue in her pocket and passed it to the girl, then stroked her hair. "Rest. I'll see you in an hour." She stood and touched Justin's shoulder as she left their room and opened the door to the room next to them.

Ninety minutes later, they were in the Eurotel bar, the same place where Bernie had sat with Karl Berset in 1978, before she slept with him and created Michael. She sighed at the memory, and when the kids looked up at her, she blushed. *I should be thinking about Gary, not Karl Berset*, she rebuked herself silently. But she did think about Karl, and how he was managing. While the kids stared down at their phones, Bernie wondered if Michael would show up tomorrow. It was a long trip from Geneva and they'd have to leave early if they were coming. Weekends were important to him, to be with his family. But if he comes, she thought, I'll ask him about Karl. And I'll find out about his genetic testing. Nicole's fingers flew over the tiny keyboard on her phone. Hopefully not texting to her friends how lame her stepmother is. Bernie had always hoped for a closer relationship with Gary's daughter; now there was an ocean between them, and she couldn't hope to bring Nicole close in just a few days.

"Okay, we have to do something." Bernie broke the silence, then she reached into her purse for Swiss francs and laid them on the table. "We can't just sit in here!" She looked at Justin and Nicole, whose blank faces registered...nothing.

"Come on, we're taking a walk. I want to show you where your dad lived. It's a nice walk." She stood and slipped into her coat. They followed her lead.

Stepping outside, Bernie was temporarily blinded, even though the sky was full of clouds. That bar was just too dark, she thought. She led the way around the corner to the start of the Boulevard de Perolles, pointing out landmarks as she walked.

"This cinema was here when we were students, although we could rarely afford to see a movie. And that tea-room, too. Amazing that after thirty years, they're still here, still the same. Back home it wouldn't be that way, right?" She turned to look at the kids, who nodded silently. Bernie stopped across the street from where she had lived.

"This is the building where I lived as a student," she said. Raising her arm, she pointed up toward the roof. "See that window? The second from the left at the top? That was my window." She lowered her arm and faced Justin and Nicole. "I lived in a tiny room that was no bigger than a small closet. It's hard to imagine, hard for me now, to think I lived in such a small place for almost a year. There was only a toilet and a cold-water sink on the floor, and I had to share it with an old woman who also lived in the attic."

"Where did you take a shower?" Nicole asked in her small, high-pitched voice.

"Well, there was an elderly couple who lived downstairs," Bernie said, pointing again at the building. "They owned the room I lived in. I had a key to their apartment, and I was allowed to enter once a day, between eight and nine o'clock in the morning, to use their bathroom for a shower."

"So if you overslept, you were out of luck," Justin mused with a slight smile.

"And that happened more than once," Bernie said, grateful that she had at least a tiny portion of their interest. "Then it was a washcloth and icy cold water!" She grinned. "Some students had full bathrooms; it depended on where they lived. I liked the fact that I had my own room, but I couldn't cook. I had one of those hot pots, you know. For tea or instant soup. But at least I had my privacy. My friend Lisa had a bigger room, but she shared the apartment with her landlady." Bernie looked beyond Justin, picturing Erika Stangl, with her tangled blonde hair, sheer, gauzy layers of clothing, gold bracelets that jingled on her tanned arm. Such a free spirit, she was, and such a trusted friend when I needed one the most.

"You couldn't cook? You must have been really skinny," Nicole murmured, casting a glance down at Bernie's wide hips.

Bernie laughed. "I wasn't, Nicole! I was *never* skinny. I might not have been able to cook, but I ate plenty. Lisa and I used to say that the four food groups were bread, cheese, beer, and chocolate." Nicole giggled at that and Bernie looked down the street. "Come on, there's a great chocolate shop down here."

They walked another block, past her old apartment building, to the Mercure shop, still the same. Its window display was filled with red hearts, and Bernie felt a stab again in her chest, remembering Valentine's Day. The kids just stared at the window, and she smiled, recalling her own first reaction to Swiss chocolate.

"We'll stop in on the way back. There's something I want to show you first," she said.

They continued down the boulevard for another ten minutes until they'd nearly reached the end. Bernie looked up and saw the sign for Rue Saint-Marc and on the corner was the high-rise apartment building where Gary had lived as a student.

"Your dad lived in this building," she said, turning her face up to gaze at the building. The sun broke through the clouds and warmed her face, as much as a February sun could warm anything.

"What floor did he live on?" Justin stared up at the building.

Bernie looked at him. "I don't know, Jus. I never was in your father's room." *I was so focused on Timmy Lyon that year that it never occurred to me to visit Gary. And he lived right down the street from me*, she thought. "He had a long walk to school. He even bought a bus pass."

She remembered walking down to this building on New Year's Eve in 1978. Lisa was sick that night, and Bernie was alone. Gary was still traveling on holiday break. If Lisa or Gary had been around, maybe she wouldn't have slept with Timmy that night. Maybe. She pictured Gary in her mind, all that shaggy hair and those wire-rimmed glasses. *"I loved you way back in Fribourg,"* he'd told her. *"But I didn't have the courage to tell you."*

Her eyes burned with the memory. *How lucky was I*, she thought. *To have had a man who loved me years ago find me, love me again. Damn it, Gary.* She swiped at her eyes, determined not to cry in front of his children.

Bernie felt hands on her shoulders first, then arms around her. From both of them. Turning, she wrapped Justin and Nicole in her embrace, and right there on the sidewalk, in front of Gary's old building, they wept.

Chapter Nineteen

Lucia had the boys dressed and ready to go by seven. Klara opted to stay home. She didn't want to miss a day visiting Bruno, believing he would know if she wasn't there, but she'd asked Michel to express her sincerest sympathies to Bernadette, and he promised he would. They took a taxi to the train station, and Lucia reminded Michel that once they were moved into the new house, they could walk or take a bus. Everything would be closer.

"Are you nervous, *amore*?" Lucia held Luca on her lap, and Jean-Bernard sat between them in the back of the cab.

"No, I wouldn't say nervous," Michel said. "I feel very sad for Bernadette. And I do wonder what she'll do now. As I understand it, Gary was a visiting professor at the university in Innsbruck, so now..." He looked at Lucia with questioning eyes.

"Who is Bern'dette?" Jean-Bernard piped up. Before answering, Michel caught a warning look from Lucia.

"She is a friend from America, *mon petit*," he

said, seeing Lucia's satisfied expression out of the corner of his eye. "The last time she came to visit, you were just a little baby."

"And I'm six years old!" He held up his hand, with all five fingers splayed out. Lucia took his other hand, unbent one finger and held it up next to the open palm.

"A big boy," Lucia murmured, stroking his head. Luca nestled against her breast, his eyes droopy. It was an early day for all of them.

The train arrived in Fribourg, and Michel walked to the ticket office to purchase tickets for the bus to Schwarzsee. It didn't leave until ten, so he made his purchase and signaled to Lucia that they should wait in the café next to the station.

"Milk for the boys," he said to the waiter. "Coffee for us. And some croissants, please. Almond and chocolate." The waiter nodded and walked away. Michel looked around the café. He'd never once been inside this place while he lived in Fribourg. Too busy, he supposed. When work ended, he hurried home. Now he sat and watched the people of Fribourg, coming and going, always with a destination in mind. Sunday was a day to travel, to visit family and friends, to do some sight-seeing. Even on a chilly February day, people still traveled on Sunday.

"Hanna!" He was jolted by Lucia's cry. Dr. Hanna Schmidt entered the café and waved to them. Michel stood as she embraced Lucia and the boys. He hugged her hard.

"So good to see you! Are you here for the same reason that we are here?" Michel asked, assuming the answer.

Hanna nodded and lowered her eyes. She glanced at the boys. Luca tore apart a croissant while Jean-Bernard took small bites.

"Such a tragedy," she said softly.

"No warning?" Lucia asked.

Hanna shook her head. "There usually isn't with a brain aneurysm, unless he had been complaining of headache, but even then..." She shuddered. "Poor Bernadette. She'll appreciate that we're here, I think. Gary's children are with her at the Eurotel." She tilted her head in the direction of the tall hotel that stood across the street.

"I didn't make a promise to her, because I wasn't sure we could come," Michel said, entwining his fingers through Lucia's. "My mother stayed back with my father," he added.

"How is he, Michel?" Hanna's words were soft.

Michel swallowed hard before answering. It was always difficult to speak about his father. But Hanna asked out of concern, he knew. "He's okay, thank you. We had him living at home with us for some time, but he receives better care now at the Maison Wagner. My mom visits with him every day. She doesn't like to miss a day."

"It's a difficult journey, Michel. I'm sorry," she said. He nodded, glad to end the conversation.

Hanna turned. "And Lucia, how is everything going? You look rested. Yes? You're doing well with the new doctor?"

Lucia nodded vigorously to all the questions. "Yes, I'm fine." She rested her free hand on her belly, its curve now showing, a promise of life. "Dr. Morales is very nice. Of course, she is not you, but she is a good doctor."

"Ah, you are accustomed to being pregnant now, Lucia!" Hanna laughed, her eyes twinkling.

The waiter returned and took the doctor's order for tea and toast.

Lucia asked, "So we'll take the bus at ten. Do you know if Bernadette and the children will also take that bus?"

Hanna shook her head. "I haven't spoken with her since Gary's children arrived yesterday. Perhaps we'll see them walk across the street. If you would rather wait and take a later bus, that's okay with me."

"No," said Lucia, "I think we should get on the bus. The boys have a lot of energy and if we arrive too early at least they can run around up at Schwarzsee."

Michel paid the bill and they walked from the café to the place where the bus waited, its engine off. They handed their tickets to the driver and found seats, Jean-Bernard seated with Michel, and Luca stayed on Lucia's lap so Hanna could sit with her.

Michel checked his watch. Five minutes to ten. Perhaps Bernadette had taken the nine o'clock bus? He didn't know if he should call her, so he leaned forward and touched Hanna's shoulder.

"Do you think we should call Bernadette? Or

send a text, just to be sure?" He was aware they'd made a long trip; he didn't want to miss seeing her after all this.

"I'll send her a quick text," Hanna said. She pulled her phone from her pocket and tapped quickly. In less than a minute she had a reply. "Oh," she said, "hold the bus, they're coming!" Hanna stood and walked to the front, where she bent to speak to the driver. He nodded and looked at his watch, then grunted something that Michel couldn't hear. Hanna returned.

"I explained the situation. He's not overjoyed, but he'll wait for a few minutes," Hanna said.

But he didn't need to wait. Michel saw the coppery curls of his birth mother as she ran across the street, accompanied by two young people: a tall boy and a tiny girl. Gary's children.

She was breathless as she climbed aboard the bus and her eyes filled when she saw Michel and his family.

"Oh, Hanna! Thank you." She embraced her old friend and touched her cheek. Turning, she introduced Justin and Nicole to Hanna, and Hanna engaged both of them in conversation while Bernie turned to Michel and Lucia. She stooped low to look Jean-Bernard in the face.

"*Bonjour*, Jean-Bernard. What do you think of this bus?" She smiled at the boy, who stuck out his little hand to touch Bernie's wet cheeks.

"Hello," he said, staring solemnly at her. "Why are you crying? Did you do something bad?"

Lucia leaned in. "This is Madame..." Lucia flushed red with embarrassment, but Bernie rescued her.

"I'm Bernadette," she said to the little boy. "And I'm very happy to see you, Jean-Bernard. The last time I was here, you were just a tiny baby."

"Like Luca?"

"Even smaller," said Bernie, demonstrating with her hands. Jean-Bernard's brown eyes were huge.

"This is Luca," Lucia said, still holding her youngest. "Bernadette, I'm so sorry," she whispered.

"Thank you, sweetheart. It was so sudden, and I think it still hasn't sunk in. But I'm very grateful you're here. It must have been a long trip for you. An early morning," she added.

"It was important to be here, together." Lucia turned to Michel, who waited patiently. He stepped around Jean-Bernard to the aisle so he could take Bernadette in his strong arms.

"I'm so sorry," he said into her hair, and she cried softly against his coat.

"Michael, my Michael, look at you," she said, pulling back. She touched his face. "How time passes so quickly." She turned, remembering Gary's kids.

"Everyone, these are Gary's children. Justin and Nicole." She turned to them. "Guys, everyone here speaks English, well, except the kids. You met Hanna, she was a good friend to me when I was a student here in Fribourg. And this is

206

Michael, er, Jean-Michel, and he goes by Michel. And his wife Lucia. And their boys, Jean-Bernard and Luca."

Michel extended his hand to Justin, who shook it. Lucia nodded to Nicole, who smiled back shyly.

Hanna moved to a vacant seat as the bus driver started the engine.

"Nicole, would you like to sit with me?" Lucia pulled Luca back onto her lap and slid toward the window so the young girl could sit next to her. Luca sucked his thumb and gazed with sleepy eyes at Nicole.

"Would you like to hold him? He's sleepy, he won't fuss," Lucia whispered, moving Luca to sit on Nicky's lap. Nicole wrapped her arms around the boy and lowered her lips to the top of his head.

Justin took a seat next to Michel, and turning to him, said, "So, you're Bernadette's son."

Chapter Twenty

It was time for Justin and Nicole to return home. The week had passed, and it seemed as though each day brought Bernadette closer to Gary's children. Up in the mountains at Schwarzsee the previous Sunday, Bernie took a walk with the kids while the others stayed in the warm café. She'd had a long conversation with them about their dad, and both Justin and Nicole agreed that Gary would not have wanted a traditional burial. There were companies that would scatter one's ashes in a ceremony (an expensive ceremony), but Bernie knew Gary would have detested something like that. So instead, she and the kids hiked into the woods and found a spot on the forest floor in a quiet area hidden by trees. They each said a prayer before burying the ashes next to a tall pine tree and covering the area with pine needles. Then they hiked back to the café, where Bernie and Gary had spent that Sunday afternoon on a spring day in 1979. This time they all sought warmth from the icy rain that had started to fall outside. Hanna had alerted the manager about their group, and he had hot soup and sandwiches ready. Through tears, there was also laughter, and a lot of love shared. Michel and Justin stayed engaged throughout the day, and little Luca clung to Nicole with such ferocity it gave Lucia pause. Nicky came to life in his presence, and Bernie wondered if she'd find a career working with children.

Before their last day, Bernie took Justin and Nicole on a walking tour of Fribourg, and there was a day spent in Bern, dinner at Hanna's, and day trips to Murten and Gruyères. Friday was for shopping, and Bernie remarked that it was a miracle all the chocolate would fit in their luggage.

"I'm so grateful to you both," she said at the airport in Zurich. "It meant everything to me that you could be here."

"It meant a lot for us, too, right, Nic?" Justin draped his arm over Nicole's narrow shoulders.

"Thanks for everything, Bernie," Nicole murmured, and Bernie noticed it was the first time she'd called her by name. She looked up at Bernie with Gary's eyes.

"I love you both," Bernie said with a tightening throat. "I just want you to know that. When I look at you, I see Gary, and I just hope we always stay close. I still don't know what I'm going to do, but I have to return to Innsbruck to clean out our stuff from the apartment."

"Your son is here. Maybe you want to be near him?" Justin said it so matter-of-factly, it caught Bernie by surprise. But there is Klara to consider, Bernie thought. And Bruno. She didn't want to be in the way; she didn't want to be an intrusion in Michael's life. Still, she'd want to be there for him when he underwent the test.

"Anyway, I guess we should go," Justin said, interrupting her train of thought.

"Right! Well, then, no goodbyes. Just see you later, okay?" She opened her arms and gave each of the children a long embrace. "Have a safe flight. Please give my best to your mom," she added. "You have my cell and email, right?" Both of them nodded and Nicole leaned in to kiss her cheek.

"Bye, Bernie. I mean, see you later." She smiled then, a genuine smile. Bernie grinned back.

She held up her hand and watched them leave, then returned to the coffee shop and ordered a cappuccino.

I have to decide. What comes next for me? She'd purchased a ticket to Innsbruck, leaving in an hour. She wanted to arrive in Innsbruck late, in the dark, and just walk to the apartment. While the kids had slept in late most mornings, Bernie made arrangements via email with the university's coordinator. He'd been very sympathetic to her situation, and let her know she could stay in the apartment until the end of the month, which was only a week away.

Hanna had made an offer. "Come stay with me, Bernadette," she'd said. "As long as you need. You have a room here anytime." They'd spoken by phone, and Bernie had expressed concern about the testing for Huntington's that Michael would be going through.

"I want to be around for him, Hanna, but I know Klara is going through so much right now. My presence might add to her burden," she'd said.

Hanna's reply had surprised her. "Bernadette, Klara doesn't know about Michel's predicament."

"What?"

"Michel and Lucia decided not to tell her. She has so much worry with her husband now, and no one knows how long he will be around. Alzheimer's robs the brain, but some people live with it for years. They both thought it best not to tell her about the test, especially since the outcome is uncertain."

"I guess I understand. It's only out of concern for her, and we're all praying he doesn't have the marker."

"So, Bernadette, you must think about your own future."

"Hanna, I can't practice law here. And I can't stay without a job, or authorization."

"You cannot practice law, okay, but you can teach. You're qualified to teach, Bernadette. I know some people; if you want, I will make some calls."

"Teach where, Hanna?"

"Here at the university. If you're interested."

"Here in Fribourg? I could teach here in Fribourg?"

"Let me make a call."

Bernie gulped air. Live in Fribourg again? And teach? She could hardly wrap her head around the possibility, and yet, the hope that bubbled up inside her was hard to ignore.

"Yes, Hanna. Thank you. And thank you for the offer to stay with you. I'll need a week to pack up the apartment in Innsbruck, but thank you."

Bernie telephoned her sister after speaking with Hanna. She'd called Joanie, and her aunt Joan, after Gary died, and insisted they not make the trip over to Switzerland. Aunt Joan's arthritis made it difficult for her to walk, much less spend hours in a cramped airplane. Joanie wanted to be with her, until Bernie explained that Gary's children were coming and she'd need to devote all her attention to them. Now, the idea of explaining to her only sister that she might stay in Switzerland for the foreseeable future gave Bernie pause. It would be a difficult call to make. But what good would delaying it do?

"Joanie? It's me. Did I interrupt dinner?" She held the phone to ear and listened. People strolled by, rolling luggage behind them, some with children in tow. Bernie watched while she listened to Joanie on the other end.

"No, they just left. I'm still at the airport in Zurich. I have a few minutes before my train back to Innsbruck....Well, I have to pack up the apartment. I have until the end of the month.....Wait, Joanie, listen for a sec, okay? I can't talk for long. I'm going to stay with Hanna for a little while until I figure things out. No, not just yet. Joanie, listen to me! There may be a job for me in Fribourg and I'm going to check it out. Yes! I'm serious. Listen, I'll send you an email later with all the details. Everything is okay...Love you, too. Bye."

Once she clicked off, Bernie exhaled a large breath she didn't even realize she'd been holding. She stopped into the little Migros market and picked up some fruit, water, and chocolate for the trip. She'd be back to Innsbruck late that evening and hoped she could sleep on the train.

***

The train pulled into Geneva and Karl flipped open his phone. He dialed Dani's number, but the call went straight to her voice mail and he didn't leave a message. Outside the train's window, it was dark. Both he and Ella were tired and cranky after a long, exhausting train ride. As they had on the way to Lisbon, they'd traveled via Paris; however, on the return trip, they arrived at Montparnasse instead of the Gare de Lyon. And their train back to Geneva departed from the Gare de Lyon. A taxi ride that took nearly an hour in crushing traffic had Karl ready to bolt from the cab and drag his luggage the remaining two kilometers to the station. With just minutes to spare, they made the train. Karl moved slowly, and Ella's patience was thin.

"I'm glad we reserved a room for the night," Ella said, her voice heavy.

"We could have traveled back, you know. It's only ten. We'd be home in another hour. Maybe I should cancel the room." Karl glanced at his watch.

"No!" she snapped. "I want to sleep in the hotel. I'm exhausted, Karl." Ella took out her compact and frowned at her reflection. She applied lipstick. "Did you call Dani?"

"She wasn't there."

"Did you leave a message? To let her know we arrived?" Karl was silent. "Well?"

"No, I didn't leave a message," he mumbled. "It's late, anyway."

Ella rolled her eyes. "Call and leave a message, please, Karl. Maybe she could meet us for breakfast tomorrow, before we head home." She clicked her compact shut and placed it inside her purse.

"You call her then," Karl muttered. He tossed the phone in her lap, where it bounced off and landed on the floor. The passengers across the aisle turned to look and Karl glared at them until they shifted their eyes away.

Ella leaned over to pick up the phone as the train squealed to a stop. She fixed her eyes on Karl and hissed, "Stop being such an ass." Still glaring at him, she opened the phone and dialed Dani's number. "*Bonsoir*, sweetheart, we're here in Geneva now. Just arrived this instant. Tired but well. Could you meet us at the hotel for breakfast? We won't be leaving until late morning, so call anytime. Love you, Dani." She snapped the phone and threw it on the empty seat next to her husband. Ella stood and donned her coat, ignoring Karl.

"I told you she wasn't there," he said, more to himself than to her.

"Just stop it," she seethed. She started for the exit, leaving him to pull on his coat and grab the smaller bag from the overhead rack.

She walked ahead of her husband. The large suitcase would remain in the station until tomorrow, as Ella had arranged for it to go with them back to Lausanne. Everything they needed for the night was in the smaller bag, which she hoped Karl had with him. A taxi stopped for her and she stood by the cab, waiting for her husband to catch up.

At the hotel, she continued to ignore him, giving the front desk clerk the information for their reservation.

"Are you going to wait for me?" he called from the middle of the lobby.

Rather than have another incident of people staring at them, Ella pressed her lips into a thin line and turned around to face him. She smiled but her eyes were cold.

Once they were in their room, she let loose.

"I've had enough of this, Karl! Stop acting like a baby and grow up. You used your disease like a crutch the entire time we were in Lisbon. Like you couldn't do anything for yourself. That's just ridiculous! You may be living with Huntington's for years, and I will stay with you through it all, but stop acting as if your grave is open and waiting for you to jump in." Her face was flushed, but her eyes now glistened with tears. Karl knew his wife. She would not cry if she could help it.

He slumped onto the bed. "You're right. You're right about it all. This was supposed to be our vacation, and I acted like a fool. All of our time together, it's time I can't get back to give to you. I'm sorry," he said, lifting his eyes to her.

She sat next to him, her hand on his thigh. His foot bobbed, as if to a snappy tune. "I know, *cheri*. I know you're frustrated with it, with everything. But I can't help you if you act like this. Because I don't *want* to help you when you act like this. You understand, don't you?"

He nodded. "Ella, I'd be lost without you."

"Okay, my love. Okay. Come, let's get out of these clothes and be comfortable. We can order food from the restaurant and have it brought up."

"I'll take you out if you want," he offered. She smiled at him.

"No, we'll stay in tonight. If Dani calls, we'll meet her tomorrow." Ella unzipped the travel bag and pulled out a pair of pajamas. "Here, bottoms for you, top for me."

"How about the other way around?" He wiggled his eyebrows at her.

***

"I have an early day," Michel whispered to Lucia before rolling out of bed.

"It's still dark," she said, her voice still

hoarse and throaty.

"Go back to sleep. I'll eat when I get to work," he said. Michel took a quick shower and returned to the bedroom to dress. Lucia lay on her back with half-closed eyes. He didn't turn on any lights, hoping she'd go back to sleep. It was barely six in the morning.

"Today you see the counselor?"

"Mm-hm," he murmured, zipping his fly and buckling his belt. He slipped into shoes and pulled a jacket from the closet. "At four. I'll be home after that. Probably around six." He moved to her side of the bed and bent at the waist. Kissing her on the forehead, he smoothed back her hair. "Sleep, angel." He turned and walked out of the bedroom.

They'd found a house, the one near the Botanical Gardens that Lucia liked so much. Klara was willing to move, too, thankfully. Michel knew that as long as she could still visit with Bruno every day, she would be agreeable. And the Maison Wagner was right on the bus route. Jean-Bernard's school was close, and the house had a small garden in back. So this morning he would tell Gamil Almazi that they would move out of the villa at the end of March.

Michel arrived at the hotel before any of the regular day-shift people. There was a skeletal staff at night, and he greeted the front desk clerk, who was surprised to see him.

"*Bonjour!*" Michel called as he walked around behind the front desk.

The clerk checked his watch, just to be sure.

"You're early today, Monsieur Eicher," said the man, easily twenty years older than Michel.

"Yes, an early meeting and a shortened day today," he said. "Has Monsieur Almazi arrived yet?"

"No, sir. He usually arrives closer to seven."

Michel looked at his watch. "Fine. I'll have some breakfast then."

"Shall I call the cook for you, sir? Will you eat in your office?"

Michel grinned. "No, that's okay. I'll surprise him, too." He lifted his hand and left.

The hotel dining room didn't open until seven, but the cook liked Michel. He was happy to serve him coffee and eggs. After his little breakfast, Michel climbed the stairs to Almazi's office. The door was open and he saw Gamil removing his coat.

"*Bonjour!*" Michel stepped to the doorway and waited.

Gamil turned and surprise registered on his face. "Michel! You're early today," he said. He looked away for a moment. "Ah, you have your medical appointment this afternoon, is that right?"

Michel had not said anything about the test. He wanted to, because he respected Gamil, but Lucia was adamant that he not divulge the information. She was worried that Michel might jeopardize his job, and besides, no one knew the outcome of the test before it was administered. Michel relented, admitting that she was probably right. And Gamil, to his credit, had not questioned him.

Michel nodded. "Yes, today at four. So, I am here early. Do you have a minute for me?"

"Of course, of course." Gamil waved him inside and pointed to a chair, then sat down and steepled his hands, waiting for Michel to speak.

Michel shifted in his chair. There was no reason to be nervous, he told himself. "You know that we, Lucia and I, we have been very grateful for the use of the villa since our arrival in Geneva. It is a magnificent house with plenty of room. But we have always wanted a home of our own, and Lucia found one she likes very much. We made an offer for it, and it was accepted last week. We would like to stay in the villa until the end of next month. Then we will move into our own home." He licked lips that were as dry as dust and waited.

"Well, this is indeed a surprise, Michel. I didn't know you were not happy in the house." He raised his hand as Michel tried to protest. "No, it is fine. Of course, you would like to have a house of your own, and perhaps closer to the hotel. It is perfectly understandable." He looked down at his fingers before looking up. Gamil's eyes were so black, Michel thought. "And your father? How is he adjusting?"

Michel stiffened. He always wondered how much Gamil knew about the nurse Ahmed. Gamil was the one who had provided Ahmed to care for Bruno, and Ahmed had neglected Michel's father to the point that he'd developed serious bed sores. He was only recently healed, thanks to the care he received now. "He's doing well, thank you," Michel answered in a tight voice.

"Good." Gamil stood up behind his desk. "Is there anything else?" His face was impassive.

"No, nothing. Thank you, sir." Michel turned and walked quickly from the office. He took the stairs back down to the lobby and shut the door to his office, wondering what that was all about. Why would Gamil care if they moved? The villa belonged to the company, he'd been told. So now it was free. And the business with Ahmed still bothered him. Gamil never apologized, never offered an explanation for the nurse's behavior, which Michel believed was criminal. Thank God he and his mother had discovered it in time. Well, better to forget about Ahmed. He was gone, and Bruno was in good hands.

At eight o'clock, Michel opened his door, just as the night clerk left, calling goodbye from the front desk. One of his daytime employees had not yet shown up, and this was the second time in as many weeks, Michel noted. I'll have to speak to her about that. He watched the elevator doors open as the morning started. Businessmen on their way to meetings outside the hotel. Tourists lounging on the luxurious furniture, scanning maps, deciding what to do, where to go. And, wait. What? Michel's gaze fixed on an elegant couple emerging from the elevator. They walked toward the dining room where breakfast was being served. Karl Berset and his wife?! Michel looked around. Where was Teresia, dammit? She burst through the doors, her hair a mess, dark circles under her eyes, Another late night, Michel guessed.

"Sorry, boss," she gushed. She stashed her belongings under the desk and straightened her clothes.

"Second time in two weeks, Teresia," he said sternly. "We'll talk about this later." He walked away from her and toward the dining room. There they were, just being seated. He hurried to them with his hand outstretched.

"*Bonjour!*" Their faces couldn't have shown more shock if it had been scripted. Michel looked from Karl to Ella and back to Karl. "It's Jean-Michel."

"So it *was* you!" Karl said, taking Michel's hand and pumping it. At the tilt of Michel's head, Karl explained. "I thought I saw you here before, recently. We stayed here before our trip to Portugal, and we just returned and stayed again last night. We travel back to Lausanne in a couple of hours. This is your hotel then." Karl beamed at Michel.

Michel blushed. "Not my hotel, Karl, but I am manager. You stayed here previously? I wish I had known." He lowered his voice to a whisper. "You won't pay for your room, for last night. Please. You are my guests. I hope everything was satisfactory."

"Everything was fine," Ella said, nodding at the waiter who brought coffee to the table. "There will be one more," she added as he poured coffee from a silver decanter.

"Oh no, I'm sorry, I cannot stay," Michel said.

"Not you, son," Karl replied. Looking over Michel's shoulder toward the doorway, he broke into a grin. "There's my girl! Dani! Over here!"

Dani? Michel froze in place as Dani Berset approached the table. "Dani, you said you wanted to meet your other brother. Well, here he is! May I introduce Jean-Michel Eicher."

Michel pivoted to look into the equally-horrified face of his half-sister.

Chapter Twenty-one

Bernie was done. There wasn't much to pack up, actually, since they really hadn't had time to purchase anything. She boxed up his clothes, keeping one more of Gary's shirts to sleep in. His watch, his class ring, she kept for Justin. And what about Nicole? She should have something that belonged to her father. Bernie selected a book of poetry by Gary's favorite poet, Mark van Doren. Inside the flap, Gary had written, "The art of teaching is the art of assisting discovery" with Van Doren's name in parentheses.

She opened the book to where Gary had laid a bookmark and read. Then she reread the lines and cried. She wondered if Nicole would understand; if not now, perhaps she would one day. What she wanted so much for Gary's children to know was that she was a better person because of their father, and that she made him happy. It had nothing to do with their mother; that was love, also, and a love that produced two beautiful children.

"Dammit, Gary," she yelled to the wall. And

the wall, stoic and impassive, stood as silent as an unspoken thought.

She packed the two large, wheeled suitcases and called for a taxi. By agreement, she left the key to the apartment in an envelope on the table. And when she closed the door to the place they'd called home for barely six weeks, she never looked back.

***

Dani was first to recover from the shock. She held out her thin arm and offered her small hand to Michel.

"Well!" she said breathlessly. "It's very nice to meet you! Jean-Michel, is it?" Michel was certain her eyelashes were trembling.

He took her hand and felt the heat on his face.

"Why so formal?" Karl joked from his chair. "Give your sister a hug!" He laughed out loud.

"Karl, shush," said Ella. "Jean-Michel is working. He wasn't expecting to meet Dani this morning."

Michel coughed. "Yes, I'm so sorry. I must get back to work. Dani, very nice to meet you." He pulled his hand back sharply and wouldn't look in her eyes.

"Jean-Michel, I will be in touch soon. We would love to have you and your family come to our home. You can meet our son Paul and his wife. And I know we would all like to meet your wife and children." Ella smiled encouragingly.

"Yes, yes, of course. Well, I should go now." He nodded to everyone and willed his feet not to run to the lobby.

Once in his office, he shut the door and leaned against it, nearly doubled over. Dani! His half-sister! He sucked air into his lungs.

There was a knock on his door. He stepped away so he could open it and there was Teresia.

"I'm very sorry about being late again today. My son was sick and I waited for my sister to arrive. I'm so sorry. It won't happen again."

Michel stared at her for a moment until he remembered. "Okay, Teresia, okay. I understand." He touched her forearm. "Okay," he said again, softly. Just please go back to work, he implored silently.

"Are you ill, boss? Can I help you? You're so pale."

"I'm fine. Really, thank you anyway."

She nodded and left. He shut his door again and slumped into his chair. *Dani is my half-sister.* Karl's daughter. Oh, my God. If anything had ever happened...he shook his head. Nothing would have happened. He didn't cheat on Lucia. It never would have happened.

He bolted upright in his chair. But Farid thinks something happened between them. And what if he has spoken with Gamil? He gripped the sides of his head, as if to keep his brain from exploding. If this information finds its way to Gamil, I'll be out of a job. Worse, Farid could use the information, as false as it is, to blackmail me. He heart beat wildly against his chest wall.

Michel picked up the telephone and dialed the number for his counselor. When the secretary picked up, he cancelled the appointment. There was no way he could deal with that today.

He needed to speak with Dani. They'd still be there, in the dining room. Filling his lungs with a deep breath, Michel headed out of his office. He passed Teresia at the front desk and gave her a supportive smile. "If your son is still sick, and you need to leave early, Teresia, let me know, please." Her eyes widened and she nodded.

He found them in the dining room, just finishing breakfast. As Michel approached their table, three faces turned to him.

"I want to apologize for having to rush off earlier," he began.

"Nonsense!" Karl's too-loud voice carried across the room. "You're a busy man. But you and your family will come to our home one Sunday for dinner? Soon?"

"Of course," Michel replied, turning to Dani. "Dani? Could I speak with you for a minute?"

"Sure," she said, rising to her feet. She followed him out the door to the lobby, away from her parents.

He led her to a quiet corner. "I'm so, so sorry. I had no idea."

"Neither did I! Papa never mentioned your name; in fact, I was going to ask him your name, but then, well, now I know. I met you as 'Jean-Michel,' but did I hear someone call you Michel?"

"Yes, either is fine. Listen, Dani, are you

going to have the test?"

"Yes, I plan to, but my brother Paul won't do it. He said he doesn't want to know. What about you?"

"Oh, I want to know. For my kids. But I just cancelled an appointment with the counselor this afternoon. I couldn't face it, not after the surprise of seeing you. I'll call later to reschedule." He hesitated; his next question was difficult. "Dani, do you work for Farid?" His eyes held hers, and she looked away, at the gleaming lobby.

"My parents think I'm a model," she whispered. "I am, but, you know…" she stared at the shiny marble floor. "It's complicated."

"I'm concerned that Farid thinks you and I have been intimate. If he mentions anything to Gamil…" He saw the fragile question in her eyes. "I work for Gamil Almazi, his brother. If an untruth is spoken, and God forbid he learns we have the same father, Dani, it would be terrible." He shook his head, not able to comprehend the disaster that would follow such a revelation.

Dani leaned forward. "I'm meeting a man this afternoon. No, not like that. Someone my father wants me to meet." She sighed. "Actually, I would like to stop working for Farid. The money is good, of course, but he has a temper." She peeked up at Michel. "It's not the job I wanted to have. Not what I started out to do." She blushed. "Papa would like me to marry. I'm too young for it, I'm only twenty, but perhaps if this man is nice to me, and I could get away from Farid." She exhaled. "I need a good reason to leave."

"Would he let you go?"

She looked down again. "I hope so. He's a stupid man, Michel. He thinks he is much more important than he is. But he is nothing, only wealthy. And I heard him say he wants to return to Saudi Arabia."

"Dani, here's my number. Call me if you need anything. Say you will." She nodded and finally looked up at him.

"I'm really glad nothing happened between us. You're a good husband to your wife."

"It's nice to know I have a kid sister." He grinned at her, just as Karl and Ella emerged to the lobby.

"So, we must be off now. Ella is anxious to return home," Karl said, shaking Michel's hand.

Ella embraced him. "I'll call you, Jean-Michel. We're looking forward to meeting your family."

"Thank you. I'm happy you stayed with us, and glad to have met you, Dani." He opened his arms to his new sister. She felt like a twig in his arms, so thin, so fragile.

Chapter Twenty-two

Michel arrived home and was greeted with a kiss that tasted like garlic. He didn't think it possible, but he loved Lucia more than he could ever express. And now, he wanted to tell her about Dani.

"You're home early, *amore.* How was the appointment with the counselor?"

Michel loosened his tie and shrugged out of his jacket. He pulled a bottle of beer from the refrigerator and poured the contents into a tall pilsner glass. After taking a long swallow, he turned his attention to Lucia.

"First, are the boys with Klara? Good, because I have a lot to tell you. It was an interesting day," he started. "I cancelled the appointment." Seeing the alarm on her face, he quickly added, "I rescheduled. Tomorrow afternoon, same time. There was a reason. Karl Berset and his wife stayed at the hotel last night. I didn't know about it until this morning, when I saw them in the dining room. They didn't know that I worked there, so it was just coincidence that we ran into each other." He reached over to take her hand. "And then, their daughter showed up to meet them for breakfast! My half-sister, Lulu. Her name is Dani, or Daniele, and she's about twenty years old. There's another child, Paul, my age. I haven't met him yet. So that was quite a surprise."

"But there was nothing bad? I'm sure it must have been quite a shock," Lucia said.

"Very shocking," Michel said, understating the situation that had transpired that morning. "Karl's wife, Ella, said she'd like to have us all up to their home one day. So you can expect an invitation may be forthcoming."

"What about Mama?"

Michel looked away. "I think we keep Mama out of all of this. Lulu, I don't like to keep secrets from her, but it would be upsetting for her. She was very welcoming to Bernadette, and I know she likes her, but with everything going on with Papa these days, Mama doesn't need anything to make her anxious. I think if she met Karl, especially with Papa sick, it would be difficult for her."

"You're right." Lucia rested her hands on her belly. "So, did you have a chance to meet with Gamil and tell him about the house?"

Michel nodded. "I saw him early in the morning. He seemed fine, Lulu. No problems. I told him we would be out by the end of next month." He took a breath. "And I think that when I see the counselor tomorrow, I'll tell her that I don't want to take the test until all of this is settled. After we've moved into the new house.

After we go to Lausanne and you meet Karl's family. I think we wait for our lives to settle down a bit, then I will have the test."

"It will settle, *amore*. Now, tell me about Bernadette. Do you know what are her plans?"

"Yes, she sent a message that she will live with Dr. Schmidt for a little while. I suppose she needs to think about everything, you know, decide what to do. Perhaps she would like to stay in Fribourg."

"We should invite her to visit before we move. This house has plenty of room. Klara would be happy to see her."

"Yes, that reminds me," Michel said. "I need to tell Mama about Gary. We never did tell her. But now that Papa is stable, I will tell her. This evening." He finished his beer. "I will walk down to see her. She comes to supper, yes?"

"If she likes," Lucia said. Klara often declined their invitation to dine, saying she'd eaten during the day. Lucia thought she was probably worn out from the boys. "Ask her to come tonight. I want her to always be welcome."

"Okay, I'll go now, and try to bring her back with me."

***

The train carrying Bernadette arrived in Geneva mid-morning. She telephoned Lucia to let her know she'd arrived, and asked about a bus to their home.

"There is a bus, Bernadette, but perhaps

you'd rather take a taxi? It would be faster."

"I'll see you soon, then!" Bernie ended the call and raised her arm for a cab.

A few minutes later, she gasped at the enormous house in front of her. Michel must be doing quite well, she mused with pride. *Good for him.* She used the brass knocker on the front door and Lucia flung it open.

"Oh, Bernadette!" she cried, embracing her tightly. "I'm so happy you're here!"

"Look at you, Lucia. You're beautiful. You're feeling okay?"

Lucia patted her stomach, now an adorable bump on her otherwise slender body. "Yes, fine. Doctor says early in June." She scrunched her shoulders up around her ears and smiled. "Come in!" She stepped aside and Bernie entered the enormous foyer.

"What a gorgeous house!" she said. "Why are you moving?"

"It's a long story," Lucia replied. "We'll tell you all about it tonight." She reached for Bernie's bag, but Bernie held tight.

"Forget about it," she said. "No heavy lifting for you."

Lucia said, "Come this way. You have your own bathroom."

Bernie dropped her bag into the bedroom just before the boys came running to greet her, trailed by Klara. She offered a warm embrace to Michael's mother and the women exchanged a meaningful look.

"I was so sorry to hear about your husband,

Bernadette," said Klara, her eyes moist. "He was a fine man."

"That he was," Bernie said. "And Bruno? How is everything, dear Klara? Is he well cared for?"

Klara nodded. "He does receive good care at the Maison Wagner," she said. "I try to visit every day. He doesn't speak anymore, but I do believe he knows when I'm there. That's why I go." She patted her hair, nearly all gray now. But it looked good on Klara, Bernie thought, remembering that she probably needed a color touch-up. Too many of her own gray hairs appearing now.

"I'd be happy to go with you, unless you think it might upset him."

"No, that would be nice, thank you. He won't know you, but I'd love to have the company. Lucia tries so hard, but with the two boys…"

"And another baby coming! God bless her," Bernie said.

Lucia brought tea to the low table, and they sipped in comfortable silence.

"Has Michel scheduled his test yet?" Bernie asked the question, then saw the horrified look on Lucia's face and bit back her words. *Damn*, she thought, *Klara doesn't know. I'm an idiot.*

"What test?" Klara asked, looking at Lucia then at Bernie.

"Oh, it's a test at work. Something about hotel management. He must have mentioned it to you, Bernadette." Lucia, sitting next to Klara, blazed her eyes at Bernie.

"He did, that's how I knew. When is it

again?" She lifted her tea cup to her face.

"Soon, I think. After we move," Lucia replied tersely. "So, Mama, what should we do today?" She turned to Klara.

Bernie wanted to kick herself. *What an idiot I am*, she scolded herself. Of course they wouldn't have mentioned the test to Klara, not with all her worries about Bruno. She hoped Lucia wasn't too angry at her; it seemed that Klara hadn't picked up on their lie.

"Bernadette said she would like to accompany me to visit Bruno," Klara said, sitting primly on the sofa with her hands clasped in her lap.

Bernie caught Lucia's warning look. She smiled. "I'll go with Klara today, if that's okay with you, Lucia."

"Sure, of course," she said, standing up. "Maybe tomorrow we can do something with the boys."

Bernie was sure she'd offended Lucia. Oh, dear, she'd just arrived. How many secrets were in this family?

"Bernadette, I will gather my things, and meet you back here in ten minutes? Or are you too tired?"

"No, not at all." Bernie stood, too, and picked up one of the trays to bring to the kitchen. "I'll be ready."

Once Klara had left, walking to the back of the house, Bernie set down her teacup on the kitchen counter. "Lucia, I'm so sorry, I didn't think before I spoke. Klara still knows nothing then about Michael's test? Or about the Huntington's?"

Lucia bit her lip. "It's okay, Bernadette, I don't think she suspected anything. We haven't told Mama about any of this. It's too much worry for her. Michel and I, we are praying for a good outcome, and I try not to think about a different result." She laid a hand over her stomach, as if to shield the unborn baby from any talk of an inherited disease.

"You shouldn't have these kinds of worries. You're both too young and full of promise. Everything will be fine." She was surprised at the intensity with which Lucia hugged her. This girl needed physical comforting, and Bernie suspected she hadn't been receiving any for a long time. Then again, it did Bernie good to have human contact, too.

***

Michel was glad to have Bernadette in his house. Lucia seemed happy and comfortable, and Bernadette wouldn't allow Lucia to do any housework. According to Lucia, once Jean-Bernard was off to school, Bernadette insisted that Lucia rest, or nap if Luca was napping, and she set about doing household chores for the next hour.

One evening, Michel arrived home to find Bernadette in the kitchen, at the stove, while Lucia read a book to the boys, nestled on either side of her. Bernie hummed to herself, content, he thought, as if she was right where she belonged. His thoughts began to slip into place, like those last pieces of a jigsaw puzzle that had until that moment been elusive.

"So, do you think you'll be teaching in Fribourg?" Michel asked later that night over coffee and cake.

Bernie shrugged. "I don't know yet," she said, breaking off a square of her favorite chocolate bar. "Hanna knows some people at the university, but even if there was a job, it wouldn't start until September. That's six months from now, and I can't be idle for that long."

"What about the university here in Geneva?" Lucia asked. Michel smiled; he knew Lucia would love for Bernadette to stay. She'd even mentioned it to him the previous evening, a whisper while they lay in bed. Lucia loved Klara as much as her own mother, but Bernadette seemed like more of an older sister. Bernadette was vibrant at fifty, Michel thought. Being around the children brought her joy, he could tell, a small antidote to the pain she felt from Gary's death.

"Yes, that would be a good idea," she said. "You see, I cannot practice law here, although it appears I could work as a legal consultant without a specific license. But I don't know international law."

"I think you should look into teaching English. You could always do this consulting work on the side. But a teacher has a better chance of staying. If you want to stay." Michel raised his eyebrows and crossed his fingers under the table.

"I don't know what I want. Honestly, I feel like a boat without an anchor, just drifting about on the lake. When Gary was offered the job in Innsbruck, it was such an exciting opportunity. And he'd just been let go from the university where he'd been a professor for years, so it was a wonderful chance for the two of us. I'm not independently wealthy, so I need to work. Perhaps teaching is the answer," she concluded, and glanced from Michel to Lucia.

"Perhaps Michel would hire you at his hotel," Klara said, as Michel's fork clattered onto his plate.

Bernie looked at Michel, whose neck had reddened. The flush crept upward to his cheeks. He's just like I am, she thought, no hiding our emotions when we blush so easily.

"Well, um, first of all, Mama, it's not *my* hotel. And I don't think Bernadette is looking for a job in a hotel." Chambermaid? Pot-washer? He was mortified that his mother would even bring it up.

Fortunately, Bernie spoke first. "No, that probably wouldn't work out," she said with a laugh, "but thank you, Klara, for thinking of me. I will look online tonight and go to the university tomorrow." She rested her chin in her hands.

After the meal was concluded and the children were put to bed, Klara said good night and retired to the back wing of the big house.

"I have a couple of telephone calls to make, so I'll leave you two for a few minutes," Michel said. He stopped on his way out of the dining room, and reached into a low cupboard. He pulled out a bottle and brought it to the table, along with a couple of small glasses. "Have a drink while you wait. I'll be back in just a few minutes."

"Well, he doesn't bring this out very often," Lucia said. "Only for special guests," she added, sliding one of the glasses away from her. "He'll have a drink with you."

"I'll wait for him to return," Bernie murmured. "Never was one to drink alone. And I'm not about to start now."

In his office, Michel shut the door and checked his watch. It was only half past eight. He picked up the phone and dialed.

Chapter Twenty-three

Karl Berset was alone in the house, insisting to Ella that he was perfectly fine by himself. He probably was lying, but he didn't want her around all the time, as if he was a child. He pulled out his phone and a pad of paper, then dialed Raphael Klug's number and spoke to his secretary.

"Good morning, Sonya. Karl Berset here. Not too bad. Well, some days are better than others. Is he in? Sure, thanks." While he waited, he printed the letters of the alphabet on a piece of paper. He got to "J" when he heard his lawyer's voice on the other end.

"Rafe! *Salut.* Fine, fine. No, no changes." He listened to his lawyer speak. "Yes, they've gone out a few times. Apparently it's working out well," he said. "Of course, she's not going to tell her father about her dates, but she seems very happy. Yes, I agree, it's a good match. Well, feel free to tell your brother that. Rafe, listen. I have a big favor to ask. No, a big one. I don't want Ella to know about this. She's out until mid-afternoon. Do you mind coming here? Yes, of course. I'll see you in a half hour." He hung up the phone and tapped his pen again, this time with excitement, not nervousness.

Twenty-eight minutes later, Rafe Klug rang the doorbell and Karl shuffled to the door to open it. He welcomed the lawyer into his house and they sat down across from each other.

"So, what's this all about, Karl?" Rafe leaned forward, elbows resting on his thick thighs.

"There's a woman, an American woman. I knew her when she was a student in Fribourg. We had an affair, a weekend fling. From that affair, she had a child, a son, my son. I've met him."

Rafe's eyes narrowed. "Is she trying to get money from you?"

"No, nothing like that. I've met the son, a good young man. In fact, I contacted Bernadette when I found out about the Huntington's Disease. Because her son needed to know. And from what I understand, he is going to be tested, to find out if he carries the marker. But that's not the favor."

Rafe leaned back in his chair. He rested his hands on his big belly. "What do you need?"

"She's here in Switzerland. Her husband died last month, unexpectedly. They were living in Innsbruck at the time; he was teaching at the university." Karl rubbed his forehead. "Her son called me last night. Presently, she's staying with him and his family in Geneva, and she would like to stay in the country if she could get a job. Maybe at the university. Something to keep her in the country." Karl licked his lips. "Rafe. I didn't do right by her. I didn't know she'd gotten pregnant, but still, she went through it by herself. This is a chance for me to do something good. I don't want her to know it's coming from me, though." He looked down. "I'm sure she still hates me, not just for the way I treated her thirty years ago, but for this damned disease. That our son might be carrying it, too, and his children.

"You didn't know, Karl. When does he take the test?"

"Soon, I believe. Dani, too. My Paul won't have anything to do with it." He shook his head at the mention of Paul. "So, is there any way you can help? Anyone you know? She's a lawyer, but Jean-Michel said she could maybe teach English or something. Anything so she can stay. Please."

Rafe took his top lip between his teeth and chewed. His eyes scanned the room, from the ceiling to the corners as he thought about it. When he finally returned Karl's gaze, he said, "Let me make a couple of calls."

"As soon as possible, please."

"Yeah, okay. For you, Karl. One of my best clients. And perhaps, my brother-in-law to be."

Karl hoisted himself to his feet and extended his hand. "I appreciate it." He lost his balance and sat down hard. Rafe laid a sympathetic hand on his shoulder.

"I'll let myself out."

***

By mid-morning the next day, Michel received a call from Karl.

"Bernadette should make an appointment with Alfred Ulmer at the university. He'll be expecting her call. Write this down, son."

Michel, sitting at his desk, took the information and thanked Karl. "Please give my best to your wife. And to Dani," he said.

"I hope everything works out," Karl said quietly. "When do you have the test?"

"After we move," Michel said. "We are in the new house next week. Probably in early April. Then I'll know. What about Dani?"

"She's having second thoughts. Now she's involved with someone and I think she's too scared to find out. Her boyfriend says it won't matter, but she's afraid that he'll leave if the test is positive."

"I understand, Karl. I'm afraid, too. Would it be okay if I called her?"

"Sure, call her. She won't mind. Maybe you can convince her. Or not. Paul still won't budge. Anyway, good luck with all of it. We'll have you to the house soon, after you're settled in the new house."

Michel thanked him again and ended the call. He was just about to dial Bernie's number when Gamil appeared in his doorway.

"We need to talk," he said, entering Michel's office and closing the door behind him.

"Sure," Michel said. An icy chill crept down his spine. Why did Gamil make him so nervous?

Gamil pulled out a chair opposite Michel

and sat. He flattened his palms on Michel's desk. Olive skin, long fingers, unadorned. He knew nothing about Gamil's personal life.

"I need to attend to some business in Dubai," he said, his black eyes fixed on Michel.

Michel nodded. "How can I help while you're away?"

"I don't know how long I'll be gone. I need you to work with McDonald, closely. See that everything runs smoothly. Fix whatever doesn't. It's your usual job. Times ten. Can you do that?" He stood up.

Michel stood as well. "Of course, sir. I wish you a safe trip." He offered his hand.

Gamil looked at it for a second longer than normal, than shook Michel's hand. "Thank you," he said, and with one last penetrating look, he was gone.

Michel sat down and wondered what that was all about. The Almazi group had property in Dubai; it wasn't unusual for Gamil to travel. It sounded as if he could be away for some time. Burt McDonald was much more relaxed and easygoing.

He dialed Bernie's cell phone number. When she picked up, he relayed the information to her and advised her to set up an appointment with Alfred Ulmer at the university, as Karl had mentioned.

"Oh, Michael, thank you so much. I don't know how you did it, but thank you."

Remembering that Karl did not want his name involved, Michel simply said, "I hope everything works out. I'll see you at the house this evening."

"I have something special planned for dinner. Lucia knows about it but she's keeping it a secret." Michel smiled at the sound of Bernadette's voice; she needed a purpose, and now it looked as though she would have one. He was happy to be able to help. And if she was able to secure a job at the university, it meant she'd be staying in Geneva.

That evening, over a traditionally Irish dinner of roast lamb, boiled potatoes and carrots, and Irish soda bread that Bernie baked that afternoon, she told them about the appointment she had with a man named Ulmer the next day.

"He was very glad to hear from me," she said, beaming at Michel. "I think something good might happen!"

"This meal is delicious," Klara said, smearing butter on a piece of soda bread.

"Well, you know I grew up in an Irish-American family," Bernie said. "Today is Saint Patrick's Day, a big day in America for anyone with Irish ancestry." Bernie wore a green sweater, to match her eyes. Lucia, who didn't own one single green item, allowed Bernie to tie a green ribbon in her hair, and Klara found a gray blouse with green accents that Bernie had pronounced as perfect for the day.

"I feel a bit out of place wearing blue," Michel said sheepishly.

"Well, you're not Irish," Lucia said, then

stopped abruptly. She glanced at Bernie, whose copper curls danced around her head.

"Everyone is Irish today," she said. "Pass the lamb, please."

Chapter Twenty-four

Bernie turned away from the early morning slant of the April sun. Taking a step to her left, she found the shadow and spoke to Michel. "I'll be fine," she said. "Hanna and I will enjoy a quiet dinner together."

Michel cocked his head to one side. "Are you sure? I don't think he would mind."

Bernie took her son's arm. "It doesn't matter. I couldn't do it. His wife, his children. I don't belong there." She pulled his arm tighter, drawing him to her. "Michael, I feel genuinely sorry for what has happened to him, but I really don't want anything to do with Karl Berset! And I'm very sure his wife doesn't want to see me. You do understand that, don't you?"

Michel nodded. "I understand, yes. It's just that, well, he's trying. Trying to right some wrongs. I think he knows his time is limited, at least his cognitive time, and he is trying to make some things right." He glanced away.

Bernie took his chin in her hand, startling him. "Did he have anything to do with my getting the job at the university?" Her green eyes locked onto his. "Tell me."

Michel squirmed under her grasp, as if he were a nine-year-old boy instead of a nearly thirty-year-old man. "Okay, okay, he made a call. But you got the job, Bernadette. You earned the job on your own."

She released him, and laid her hand against his cheek. "I suspected as much. You called Karl and Karl called someone. You did this because you love me. Karl did it because he loves you. It's fine, Michael. Thank you." She kissed his cheek and wiped away the lipstick imprint that she left there. "Happy Easter. Klara will be with Bruno?"

Michel nodded. "She wouldn't have it any other way, you know that."

"And does Karl know about the test results yet?"

Again he shook his head. "I was very vague about the date. So I can share the good news today." He caught his breath. "I'm so relieved. For my children."

Bernie's blinked back the sting of tears in her eyes. "I was so worried, Michael. And what about Dani?"

He shrugged. "Last time I spoke with her, she didn't think she'd go through with it. She has a boyfriend, and maybe she'd rather not know. It's her decision. Karl's son Paul refuses to have the test. Even with a baby coming." He caught one of her tears with his thumb. "All I know is that I had to do it, for my boys, for the little girl coming soon. And now just knowing they'll never have to worry about it..." he choked on the last words.

Bernie took him in her arms. "No worries, my boy. My beautiful boy." She stepped back as the train pulled into the station. "I love you so much."

"I love you, too," he said. "Enjoy your day with Hanna. Give her our love."

Bernie climbed aboard with one last wave, and Michel turned back to walk home. He had a few hours before he and his family would take a train to Lausanne, to have Easter dinner with Karl and Ella, Dani and Darek, Paul and Sophie. A house full of people, he thought. Klara was insistent about spending Easter with Bruno, and a pang of guilt tugged at Michel. But his father was gone, lost to him now. Still, he didn't want to hurt his mother. Even with the good results, he hadn't mentioned the test to his mother. Better that way, he thought.

He'd been so overjoyed at learning that he didn't carry the gene that he'd wanted to shout it from the tops of every building in Geneva. Lucia cautioned him not to appear too exuberant in front of his mother, unless he wanted to explain to her the entire story. Michel agreed. So he celebrated with Lucia in a special, intimate way. Their children would not be carriers. There would be no more talk about Huntington's.

Back home, he asked Lucia for one small favor and she readily agreed. Since everyone was dressed from church services earlier that morning, he led them to Klara's room at the back of the house. She was just about to leave for the

Maison Wagner when they appeared in her doorway.

"Have you come to say goodbye?" She adjusted her new pink hat. Michel was pleased to see his mother fuss with her appearance. He knew she wanted to look good for his father.

"We're coming with you, Mama," he said, kissing his mother's cheek and offering his elbow.

"What? What about your dinner in Lausanne?" Klara had been shocked to learn that Michel was taking Lucia and the boys to dine with the man who had fathered him. Without divulging anything about Karl's disease, Michel simply explained that he had asked Bernadette about the man's identity, just to know. He was nonchalant and said that it was time they met. She accepted his statement, although Michel thought she looked confused and a bit sad.

"They don't expect us until early afternoon, Mama," Lucia said. "We'll all go visit with Papa."

Klara's smile matched the sun in a cloudless sky, and Michel knew they had made the right decision. As much as he loved Bernadette, and as much as he had grown to like Karl Berset, Klara Eicher was his mother. He would do anything for her, always.

They all rode the bus to the Maison Wagner. True, Bruno showed no sign of recognition. He stared past each of them, even Jean-Bernard and Luca when they ran to him, calling "Nonno!" But he was clean and dressed for the day. Michel had no idea what was left of his father's mind, but he held his hand, stroked his hair, and sat alone with him reciting a prayer that Bruno had taught him years ago.

Klara stayed on to visit longer, telling Michel she'd take a bus back to the house, and wished them a good visit.

Now, as they stood on the platform waiting for the train that would take them to Lausanne, Michel held little Luca's hand and Jean-Bernard held on to his mother's. In her free hand she grasped a bunch of flowers, and Michel held a bottle of wine in a long, thin bag. He recalled how easy it was to have Bernadette with them; she always took one of the kids. But soon Jean-Bernard wouldn't need someone to hold his hand. The time flew by so quickly. Next month Michel would turn thirty, and he couldn't believe it. Where had the years gone? There was no time to dwell on a possible answer, as the train pulled up with a screech of brakes. Jean-Bernard pulled his hand from Lucia's to cover his ears.

"Come on, now, climb up," Lucia instructed, one hand on Jean-Bernard's back. The little boy took giant steps into the train's compartment and jumped into a seat. "Here, Papa!" he cried.

Michel sat next to his son, allowing Jean-Bernard a view out the window. Lucia sat across from Michel, their knees touching. He rubbed his shin against hers, and she smiled up at him through her lashes. Luca pressed his nose to the window, in awe of the station and all the people.

From the Lausanne station, it was a short walk to the Berset house. Michel hadn't forgotten how to get there; it was only months ago that he had shown up at their door.

He pressed the doorbell and they waited. Michel breathed air that was filled with springtime promise - new life, regeneration. The door was opened by a man he'd never met, but who he knew had to be Paul Berset.

He was surprised, however, by the scowl on his half-brother's face.

"Well, come on in, then," Paul barked, stepping to the side and frowning at the boys.

Ella dashed to the door, wiping her hands on her apron.

"Welcome! *Bienvenue!*" she said. "Let me take your coats." She held her hands out for Lucia's light coat, for Michel's jacket.

Michel kissed Ella's cheeks and offered the bottle of wine. Lucia held out the flowers.

"Oh, you're so kind," she said. "That wasn't necessary." She took the flowers and the wine and set both on the kitchen counter. "Michel, it's good to see you again." She held out her empty hand. "And Lucia, it is a pleasure to meet you." They held hands and Ella looked down. Her face split into a wide grin when she saw the boys, and she stooped down to their level.

"Hello," she said solemnly, and the boys stared in wide-eyed wonder at the pretty lady before them.

"We might have a kitten soon," Jean-Bernard said. "And I'm six."

"A kitten! That would be wonderful!" she said, and Michel could see she was clearly comfortable with the boys. She turned her face to Luca. "And what is your name?"

Lucia started to answer for her son, but Michel held up a finger, waiting for Luca to respond. He did, in a barely audible whisper.

"Luca," he mouthed to Ella, who repeated, "Luca! A marvelous name!" And with that, Ella owned the two boys for the day. They would have followed her anywhere, especially after she offered each of them a cookie.

"Only one, please," Lucia said. "Not to spoil dinner."

Ella rose. "I'm sorry, I should have asked you first."

"No, it's fine. Thank you," she added. They were still standing in the entryway.

"Please! Come in," she ushered them into a large living room, where Paul sat on the sofa next to a woman Michel assumed was his wife, Sophie. She was as pregnant as Lucia, and smiled at Lucia when she saw that they had something in common.

"I guess you two might have some things to talk about," Ella said, as Sophie made room for Lucia at the end of the sofa. Meanwhile, Paul sat with his arms folded across his chest. Michel looked around for Karl, or Dani. Seeing neither, he walked into the kitchen.

"May I help you with anything?" he asked.

"No, Jean-Michel, thank you, though. Sit and talk with me," she said, gesturing to one of the barstools at the counter. Michel perched on the edge.

"Please call me Michel if you like. Is Dani coming?" he asked as casually as he could.

"Yes, yes, with her new boyfriend." Ella turned from the sink and took a few steps closer. She lowered her voice to a stage whisper. "We really like him. He convinced her to quit that modeling job. It took up too much time." She looked away for a moment and Michel caught a flicker of heartache in her eyes. When she turned back to him, it was gone, replaced by her bright smile.

Just then Karl lurched into the living room. Michel slid off the stool to make introductions.

"Karl," he said, shaking Karl's outstretched hand, "this is my wife Lucia, and our boys, Jean-Bernard and Luca." Karl's lips twisted into a crooked smile.

Lucia rose to shake his hand. He kissed both cheeks. "So nice to meet you, my dear," he said, and ruffled the hair on the boys' heads. "Jean-Bernard and Luca? Good names," he said, nodding. "How about a drink? Beer? Wine? Something for you, Lucia?" He ignored Paul, Michel noticed. Sophie seemed lost, torn between a loyalty to her husband and wanting to please her in-laws. He didn't envy her at all. And he wished Dani would show up.

As Karl made his way to the kitchen, Michel noticed a slight hitch in his gait. He wondered when that had come about, and how quickly the disease was progressing. Ella had everything under control in the kitchen, and Michel couldn't remain seated. He patted Lucia's hand and followed Karl into the kitchen.

Lucia and Sophie spoke in quiet voices, with an occasional soft laugh from one or the other. Michel wondered why Paul even bothered to show up if he was so miserable.

He was glad to hear a rap on the front door. It opened and in came Dani with her boyfriend, a tall, handsome man in a finely-tailored suit. Michel was glad he'd stayed in his church clothes. Paul probably didn't own a suit.

"Michel! Happy Easter!" Dani embraced him just like a sister would do.

"Happy Easter to you, too, Dani. Come, meet my wife and sons." He held her hand and brought her to Lucia. Michel watched the two women carefully, looking for any sign of discomfort from his wife, but she was relaxed, happy, and seemed perfectly comfortable in this house. He exhaled, and turned to Dani's companion, Darek. They chatted for a bit until Ella announced that dinner was ready.

Michel smiled at Dani. She looked good. Healthier, happier. She and Darek made a very fine couple, Michel thought.

"I'm really glad you could come up to join us," Dani said to Lucia. "You look wonderful! How do you feel?"

"I'm feeling good. This will be my third, so I guess I'm used to it by now," she said with a laugh. "And Sophie and I are due within weeks of each other." Lucia grinned at Sophie.

Ella stood at the head of the table, next to Karl, and held a long carving knife in her hand.

With just the slightest hesitation, she turned to Paul. "Would you, please?"

"Sure," Paul grunted, pushing back his chair. He stood, towering over his mother, and took the knife from her hand. It gleamed under the light. He plunged a large fork into the roast and began shaving off slices that he transferred to a platter.

"Jean-Michel," Karl said in a voice loud enough for the neighbors to hear. "Have you had the genetic test yet?"

***

Bernie arrived in Fribourg and saw Hanna from the train's window, pacing on the platform. There was not much activity on this Easter Sunday.

"I'm so glad to see you," she cried as she descended the train. "And I'm starving, just so you know."

Hanna laughed, that crystal, sparkling laugh Bernie remembered, and suddenly she was struck by the thought that she'd known Hanna for thirty years. They linked arms, just as Bernie and Lisa had done as students. As they made their way out of the station, Hanna said, "Starving! Well, I'm not cooking today. I made reservations for dinner. Are you okay with that?"

"Hanna, I wouldn't care if we ate at the McDonald's on the rue de Lausanne! Well, wait, I would mind that. You're not taking me there, are you?"

Hanna rolled her eyes. "I should take you

there. No, there's a lovely restaurant in the *basse-ville*. Would you mind Italian food on Easter Sunday?"

"Mind? It's a perfect idea," Bernie said. She pulled Hanna's arm closer and they set off down the street.

Chapter Twenty-five

All eyes turned to Michel. Even Paul suspended carving, holding the knife in mid-air, like a silver bird surveying its prey, until he set it carefully on the table.

Michel squared his shoulders and took a breath. "Lucia and I want to thank you for your welcome and your generosity," he said. He glanced at Dani, then looked at Lucia and saw in her light blue eyes the encouragement to say what he wanted to say. "I had the test." He looked at Karl, whose lower lip had dropped and appeared to be trembling. "I'm clear," he stated. "I don't carry the gene."

The table erupted with whoops and great sighs, from Karl and Ella, and Dani and Darek, even from Sophie. Paul, the only one not seated, stared at him.

"That's wonderful news," Dani cried. She looked at Darek and took his hand, then continued. "I'm going to have the test, too. We decided together. Next week." She exhaled loudly. "Fingers crossed," she added, holding up both hands with her fingers crossed. Darek draped his arm around her thin shoulders.

"Whatever the result," he said, locking eyes with Karl, "I will take care of Dani. No matter what." He leaned over to kiss her cheek.

"Well, I'm not doing it!" Paul erupted. "You can all go to hell!" Without a word, or even a glance to Sophie, he stormed out of the house, slamming the door behind him.

No one said anything for several seconds as the moment registered. Sophie pushed back carefully and braced her hands on the table as she stood. "I'm sorry," she said in a ragged voice. "He's not been himself lately. I should go." She stopped to kiss Ella and Karl at the table before she picked up their coats and slipped out the door.

"That man was very angry," Jean-Bernard said to Luca. "And you're not supposed to slam the door. Mama said."

Michel squeezed his eyes shut until he heard Ella laugh. Surprised, he looked at her.

"Jean-Bernard is right," she said. "You're not supposed to slam the door." Ella shrugged. "I'm sorry. Paul is having a hard time with all of this." Mostly to Dani, she added, "Your father and I have asked him too many times. He must come to the decision by himself. And he knows we will always be here for him, no matter what the future holds. But we still have to eat." She picked up the knife and sliced more meat from the roast, then passed the platter to Lucia.

Karl fidgeted in his chair. "In spite of my son's outburst and behavior, it is really a wonderful thing," he said, "to have you here today. Sophie will bless us with a grandchild in just a couple of months. I pray that all of them – Paul, Sophie, and the baby, will be healthy." He raised his glass of mineral water. "To my darling daughter Daniele and to Darek, you both fill my heart with pride. Darek, you are a good man."

As his arm began to twitch, Karl lowered his glass but continued speaking. "And to Jean-Michel and his wife Lucia. Jean-Michel, I didn't even know about you until recently, but you are a fine young man." Karl cleared his throat. "I know this disease has caused all of you great concern, because of its nature and its...persistence. I am so sorry for all of your worries, and although I'm not a man who prays regularly, I have offered prayers that each of you is spared." He bowed his head and said nothing more. Michel watched as his head continued to bob up and down, as if his neck was a spring.

"Blessings at Easter," Ella cut in, raising her glass.

***

Bernie had a good day, a warm sun in the gloominess that had defined her life since Gary died. Her sister said it would get better, but what did Joanie know? She simply grew accustomed to the emptiness, learned to live within it. At night, she'd talk to him as if he were still there. In the morning, she'd remember that a new day had begun and he was still gone. Better? Probably not, Bernie thought, at least from her perspective. But life hadn't stopped because Gary died. And this day, this warm day with the promise of spring and new life, was less bitter than the days immediately following his death.

Gary had appeared in her life twice, first as a well-mannered, respectful student, a classmate who was always kind, who, in his own words, loved her even when she wasn't available to love him back. Then he re-entered her life, after she'd made peace with her past, with Timmy Lyon, with the shame of her unplanned pregnancy, the guilt that followed after she gave up Michael for adoption. They found each other again. Gary offered his love when she was ready to accept it. And together they shared five happy, memory-filled years. They rarely argued, seeing life through the same eyes, both with an optimistic, glass half-full attitude. She was grateful to have had even a short time with Gary, because she knew he had made her a better person.

But, she thought, there wouldn't be any more men to fall in love with. She'd had Gary, and no one could ever live up to him. When she said this to Hanna, Hanna smiled.

"This was me, Bernadette, after Fred died. Fred was my bright star." She tilted her head back as they strolled to the train station. The still sky was inky black. "He is still my bright star, in the heavens."

"Hanna, I couldn't have asked for a better day today. When I return to Fribourg, I take comfort in the familiar. Thank you for dinner.

Come to Geneva soon so I can repay the generosity."

"I will. It's been a long time since I was there."

"Well, let me know. I'll call Michael; he'll get you a nice room at the hotel." She smiled at her friend. "Hanna, I've known you for thirty years. I don't think I have any other friends that have lasted as long as you have."

"You were someone special, Bernadette. I knew that the first time I met you. Fred knew it, too. I couldn't have told you then that we'd still be friends, but I'm glad we are. And I'm very happy that you've decided to stay in Switzerland."

"That's thanks to Michael. He didn't want to admit it, but he called Karl on my behalf. And Karl, well, Karl wants to make things right in his life, I think, while he still can. He'd never want me to know what he did. I'm grateful to both of them. Without Karl, I wouldn't have had Michael, so I should be thankful to him for that."

"You have a good trip back. I hope everything went well at the Berset home today," Hanna said.

"I hope so, too. I'm sure I'll hear all about it. The important thing is, Michael doesn't carry the gene. He'll never have to worry about Huntington's, not him, not his children."

Hanna leaned closer. "Listen, don't tell Lucia, but her doctor phoned me. I'm going to assist with the birth, as long as it's not a last-minute thing."

Bernie grinned. "Well, just plan to come down around her due date. Stay at the hotel, or stay with me. She'll be thrilled that you'll be there."

"Just don't tell her, in case something comes up. You know, I have pregnant women here, too." Her dark eyes twinkled. They hugged goodbye and Bernie stepped toward the train before turning back.

"Trains have been very symbolic in my life, you know. Here and at home. Neither Gary nor I owned a car. But there is always something coming or going with a train. They mean happiness and they mean sorrow." She waved to Hanna and disappeared inside. Hanna raised her hand once more and the train pulled away.

Chapter Twenty-six

Bernie and Lucia, with Klara's help, planned a thirtieth birthday party for Jean-Michel, to be held at the hotel. Gamil Almazi had relocated to Dubai and Burt McDonald had stepped in as Michel's boss. Lucia asked if they could hold a small party after hours for Michel's birthday and Burt, who was relieved to have an easygoing partner like Michel instead of the temperamental Gamil, agreed enthusiastically.

It was Monday, and Bernie had two classes to teach, one at eleven and another at three. She promised to come to the hotel as soon as her afternoon class ended. Lucia had a young woman come to the house to babysit, a girl the boys knew well and liked very much. She'd bring the boys to the hotel around six, then take them home and get them to bed.

Hanna couldn't get away, as she had three deliveries that week, all C-sections. "So many babies in May," she'd exclaimed over the phone to Bernie. "But I will be down next month for Lucia's delivery, and I'll see you then," she said. "Please wish Michel a very happy birthday from me. I remember the day from thirty years ago, just as clearly as if it had happened last week," she added.

"Me too," Bernie said.

Klara made her daily visit with Bruno a little earlier that day, and was eager to help at the hotel that afternoon. McDonald made sure that Michel was busy all day, and kept him away from the second-floor conference room.

Lucia called Ella Berset to invite her and Karl to the party.

"Oh, dear Lucia, I'm so sorry that I'll not be able to attend. My husband hasn't been feeling well lately, and I think the trip could be too much for him." Ella hadn't seen any reason to even tell Karl about the party. She knew Bernadette was now living in Geneva. She knew Bernadette had lost her husband recently. And she could think of no reason for Bernadette to be in the same room as she and Karl. Ella had long since let go of the bitterness she harbored. She didn't hate Bernadette, of course not; she felt nothing toward the woman.

Dani and Darek were going to the party, and Ella knew that Dani couldn't wait to share her news with Michel. Her test results came back and she was clear. No Huntington's for Dani. Ella had fallen to her knees when Dani burst through the door last week with the news. Karl had broken down and wept uncontrollably. And Darek was ecstatic. Ella knew Darek cared for Dani, but if the results had been different, if she'd been marked as a carrier, Ella knew it would have impacted their lives. Now, it wouldn't surprise her if he proposed soon.

As for Paul, well, Ella knew there was nothing she could do. He was sullen and withdrawn. Sophie confided to Ella that Paul was convinced he had the gene, for what were the odds that all three of Karl's children had escaped the bad luck? When Paul learned about Dani, he'd disappeared for hours, leaving Sophie and an inept teenager to manage the tattoo shop. He'd had more angry outbursts, and though he'd never touched Sophie, the tirades had frightened her so much that she'd moved in with her parents until the baby was born. Paul was alone, and Ella had tried to reach out, but it was futile. All she could do was continue to love him, pray for him, and hope that he'd realize how precious life was.

***

Bernie arrived at four-thirty, sneaking past the front desk and running up the stairs to the second-floor conference room. She knocked four times, per Lucia's request, and when the door was opened, Bernie gasped. Lucia and Klara had transformed the drab, plain room into a tropical island paradise. They'd pushed the table against a wall and covered it with some kind of grassy material. All the colors around the room were bright and festive. Even the air smelled like coconuts.

"This is fabulous," Bernie cried, clapping her

hands together. "You've done a terrific job!" Klara beamed and Bernie embraced her tightly. She looked around. "Where are the boys?" she asked.

"With the babysitter. They'll be by around six to wish their Papa a happy birthday," Lucia said, tossing a lime green lei over Bernie's neck.

"Okay, well, put me to work. I'm ready." Bernie removed her jacket and hung it over a chair.

For the next hour and a half, they set out the food (the hotel kitchen was very accommodating for their favorite colleague), strung streamers, arranged seating, and programmed music. At ten minutes to six, everything was ready. More guests arrived and stood around tall tables with drinks from the bar set up along the far wall.

A few minutes after six, Burt McDonald telephoned Michel and asked him to stop by the office before he left work. Michel cleared up his paperwork and stopped at the front desk.

"I'm just heading upstairs to see the boss, then I'm done. Have a good night," he said to his secretary.

"Same to you!" As soon as Michel had disappeared, she called the conference room. "He's on his way to Monsieur McDonald's office," she whispered excitedly.

"He's on his way!" Lucia called out. "Everyone please keep your voices down." She put the music on mute and the room quieted immediately. Even the boys were still, sensing that something special involving their daddy was about to happen.

A few minutes later, the door to the conference room opened and as soon as the guests saw hair the color of carrots, they screamed, "Surprise!"

Burt McDonald gently pushed Michel into the room, which by now not only looked tropical, but had the same temperature. Michel, at a loss for words, stood slack-jawed in the midst of forty or so friends and co-workers. Klara placed a red lei around his neck and kissed both cheeks.

"Happy birthday, my darling boy," she said into his ear. "I'm so very proud of you."

Lucia walked up and placed a yellow lei around his neck. "Happy birthday, *amore. Ti amo.* You are my light." She kissed him on the mouth as the guests clapped loudly.

Bernie eased up to Michel with a bright blue lei in her hands. As she placed it over his head, she took his chin in her hand.

"You, Michael, are the best thing that ever happened to me. You know that, don't you? Somehow I knew I would come back to you. But only when the time was right. I'm a lucky woman to be so welcomed into your family, by your mother, by your wife, and by your beautiful children. I'll never forget the day you were born. Happy birthday, my boy," she whispered to him.

There was a commotion at the door as Dani and Darek burst through.

"Late as usual!" Michel said with a laugh, seeing his half-sister. She ran up to him, like a gazelle, into his waiting arms.

"Happy birthday, Michel!" She hugged him hard, planting a dark pink kiss on each cheek.

Michel took her by the shoulders and held her back so he could look in her face. "Dani?" His soft brown eyes searched hers. He waited and bit his lip as the party continued on around him. He was oblivious to the noise and only waited to hear what he hoped to hear.

She nodded, and blinked back tears. "I'm clear," she said, choking on a sob. "No gene."

Michel pulled her back in for a long embrace and looked at Darek, who gave him a thumbs up. He turned his gaze to Lucia, who held a hand over her heart, and finally to Bernie, who pressed her palms together and looked to the ceiling.

"Happy birthday to me," he breathed.

THE END

ABOUT THE AUTHOR

Martha Reynolds ended an accomplished career as a fraud investigator and began writing full time in 2011. Her debut novel, *Chocolate for Breakfast*, was named 2012 Book of the Year in Women's Fiction by the readers of Turning the Pages Books. Its sequel, *Chocolate Fondue*, was released in March 2013. *Bittersweet Chocolate* is the third and final book in the series.

Bits of Broken Glass was the author's third novel and centers around a twenty-five year high school reunion. She is presently conducting research for a new book that will incorporate her grandfather's journal from a two-week canoeing and camping trip on three rivers in Rhode Island and Connecticut, and hopes to release the book in June 2014, to mark the 90th anniversary of the journey.

She and her husband live in Rhode Island, never far from the ocean.

Connect with Martha:
Facebook:
https://www.facebook.com/MarthaReynoldsWriter
Twitter: https://twitter.com/TheOtherMartha1
Follow my blog: http://MarthaReynoldsWrites.com

Also by Martha Reynolds

Chocolate for Breakfast

Chocolate Fondue

Bits of Broken Glass

All titles are available in print and digital
formats, through Amazon.